Brook Trout Blues

Glenn,

I hope you'll never
get the Brook Trout "blues"!

Best Regards,

Bob Romano

That's the way that the world goes 'round
You're up one day and the next you're down
It's half an inch of water and you think you're gonna drown
That's the way the world goes 'round.

—From *"That's the Way That*
the World Goes 'Round"
by John Prine

Brook Trout Blues

a novel by
Robert J. Romano, Jr.

BIRCH
BROOK
PRESS

First edition
Library of Congress Control Number: 2014950557
ISBN: 978-0-9915777-2-9

Cover art by John Swan
Original map and art details by Trish Romano
Editor: Lauren Kuczala

That's The Way That The World Goes 'Round
Words and Music by John Prine
© 1985 BIG EARS MUSIC, INC. and BRUISED ORANGES MUSIC
All Rights Reserved. Used by Permission.
Reprinted by permission of Hal Leonard Corporation

Printed and published in the United States:

Birch Brook Press
PO Box 81
Delhi, NY 13753

birchbrook@copper.net
(607) 746-7453

To view a complete list of other books by Robert J. Romano, Jr. and other Birch Brook authors, you are invited to visit: www.birchbrookpress.info

Acknowledgments

Writing is a solitary business. The writer, shut up in a room, pecks at the keys, stringing words like breadcrumbs, forming a sentence and then another. Doubt hangs alongside this uncertain trail like Spanish moss from the tops of trees. Meanwhile, the sun shines, trout rise, and while a spouse may look in from time to time, the children grow like weeds in an untended garden.

At the end of his journey, the writer wonders if others will take the time to follow, and if they do, will they enjoy the little surprises found along the way? Will they smile at that silly string of alliteration just over the rise or appreciate the wordplay hidden beside the moss-colored boulder?

For me, one of the pleasures of writing is the people I meet—both on and off the page. I am grateful to John Swan for once again providing the cover art for this novel and to John Prine for sharing his lyrics.

I'm most thankful for the support expressed by those of you I've met at fly fishing shows, book readings and T.U. meetings, and for those with whom I've had the opportunity to spend some time together on the water.

Trish and I are thankful to Wayne Seaman, who was one of the first of many to lend a helping hand, and the guys at Koob's Garage for managing, against all odds, to keep our vehicles on the road.

A special thank-you to Mike Alick and Sue Cushman as well as the many other people of Oquossoc and Rangeley, and to the owners of Bosebuck Mountain Camps, Mike and Wendy Yates, all of whom have been there whenever we were in need.

And to Trish—Lord knows why she puts up with this old fool—all my love.

ABOUT THE AUTHOR

Bob Romano lives in the northwest corner of New Jersey with his wife, Trish, and "the best puppy in the world," their Labrador retriever, Winslow Homer. Trish has contributed artwork and maps to each of her husband's books. For more than thirty years they have maintained a camp in the Rangeley Lakes Region of western Maine, which is where they spend much of their free time.

You can obtain more information about Bob's books, stories and essays by going to his website: *forgottentrout.com*

Also by Robert J. Romano, Jr.

Fishing with Faeries

Shadows in the Stream

North of Easie

West of Rangeley

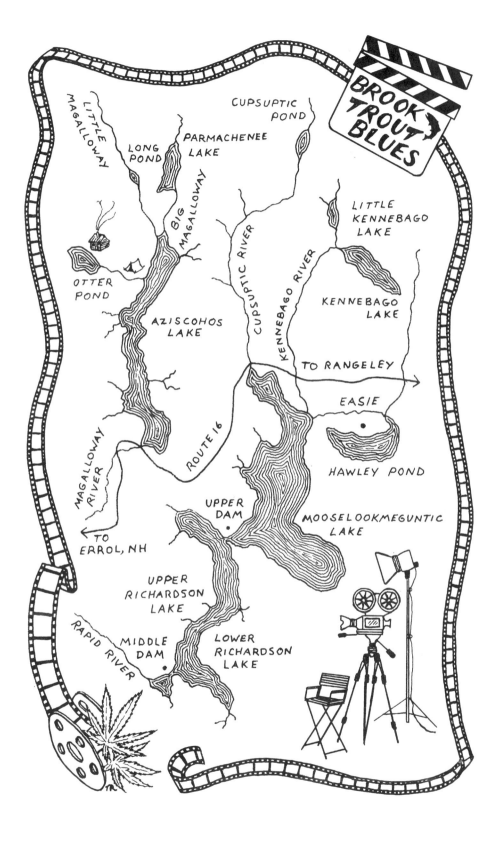

Chapter One

"Everything's gone to shit." Rusty Miller lowered a mug that contained an empty shot glass and pushed it across the rough surface of faded oak, the bill of his cap pulled down hard over his brow.

"True dat," Richard Morrell replied.

Betty Leonard frowned as she nodded her head in agreement. Ample cleavage plunged down between the three top buttons that she had left open on a dark purple blouse, her shapely breasts held in check behind the shiny, not-quite-silk material. Betty spent mornings behind Doc Treadwell's reception desk while waitressing afternoons at the Wooden Nickel, but even with two jobs she could no longer cut it, what with her husband, Roger, laid up with a broken leg and no medical insurance—which is why, on this Tuesday night, Betty, after being on her feet all afternoon, stood behind the small bar that was set back in one corner of the Nickel's cavernous room.

The waitress poured another draft for the owner of Lakeview Sports, and after filling a clean shot glass with whiskey, she turned her weary eyes to the man seated to his right.

"I'm good." The Wabanaki raised the bottle of Budweiser in his big paw of a hand and drained the few remaining drops of dark amber from the longneck. He pulled out a wallet secured to the hip pocket of his green work pants by a long metal-linked chain. Morrell's stomach pressed against a shirt that was the same color as his pants. Standing no more than five feet, eight inches, the Native American patted Rusty on the back.

"Long day tomorrow. Best I head home," he said, sliding a number of dollar bills across the top of the bar.

Nodding in my direction, Morrell zipped up a bomber jacket and pulled a pair of rawhide gloves from his back pocket. Slipping them over his gnarled fingers, he turned and walked away from the little island of light, his black leather work boots clumping against the Nickel's wooden floor. The Native American's hair swung down below his shoulders in a long ponytail. Before he faded into the shadows, a Vargas-like pinup winked at me from the cracked leather on the back of his jacket.

A moment later I heard the door of the roadhouse creak open and then slam closed, and a few moments after that the tires of the Wabanaki's pickup spinning across the parking lot gravel. Betty looked in my direction, but turned to the customers at the other end of the bar when I slipped the palm of my hand over my glass. The waitress may have looked like she was in her early thirties, but tonight those eyes betrayed her true age.

Outside, a cold rain pelted the Wooden Nickel's roof. Snow mixed with the rain, created the slushy slop that Rusty and I had slogged through earlier in the evening. Collars up around our necks, we trudged the short distance from the guide's sporting goods store, bits of the icy precipitation caught in the dull light cast by the streetlamps that hunkered over the main street of the little town. Although it was the last week of April, a string of multicolored lights remained suspended over the roadhouse door, blinking on and off in a vain attempt to brighten the gloom.

Two-and-a-half hours later I continued to nurse my second beer while trying to recall when Rusty had switched to boilermakers.

The guide remained hunched over the wooden bar that Alex Drummel had retained when he converted the hamlet's only tavern into a roadhouse that served meals from the break of dawn until ten in the evening. Alex, a refugee from the Woodstock Nation, had bought the place for cash earned from stock he purchased when a little-known software company went public. Back then no one knew the name of the company's founder, a computer geek by the name of Bill Gates.

At the other end of the bar, five or six younger guys drank beers while watching the Red Sox take an early-season game from the Yankees.

A former roadie for Jefferson Airplane, Alex had retained his contacts in the music industry, and on selected nights tables and chairs were pushed aside while live music, mostly blues, folk and bluegrass, filled the large room. Like the rest of us across the country, the middle-aged entrepreneur watched as the Washington politicians bailed out the big bankers, leaving the rest of us to fend for ourselves. Forced to cut back on expenses, he no longer could afford to book acts on a regular basis.

On those nights when music was not playing, the Nickel's little bar was no different than any other small-town watering hole—a dark alcove that smelled of stale beer, a place where ordinary men, desperate to escape their concerns, could hide out, if only for an hour or so. Most evenings the usual suspects dropped by, some to enjoy a quick beer before heading home to the family, others staying long enough to catch a bit of hockey or football on the flat-screen television Alex installed during the boom years that followed 9/11, a few hunched over shots until closing time.

Tonight the large dining room remained dark except for a single light that hung from the ceiling above the bar. Below the light, the bar's oak counter glistened under the damp rag that Betty wiped across its sticky surface. Outside the light's glow, the dark lump of our wet coats spread across a nearby table like the hill rising above the cabin that I call home from ice out to first snow.

I didn't recognize any of the guys huddled at the other end and figured they'd driven up from Farmington or Bethel with the expectation of live music, hanging around to watch the game. Betty swapped their empty beers for new ones and was refilling their bowls with beer nuts as they cheered the Boston pitcher who struck out another Yankee hitter.

"Must be nice not to have a care in the world," Rusty muttered as he stared down the bar. While walking into the roadhouse, we had passed an expensive SUV and a sporty-looking sedan, the guide complaining that they couldn't belong to anyone we knew.

He lowered his eyes toward the shot glass that Betty had filled.

Like the waitress, most people living in little towns across western Maine worked more than one job to make ends meet. Those of us who choose to live along the rivers and rills scattered throughout the pinewood forest rarely complain, figuring our way of life is preferable to most, but lately things had indeed "gone to shit."

"You've been behind in your mortgage payments before and the bank's always extended your loan." I'd been trying to reason with Rusty since we first walked in together, but rather than answer he lowered the shot glass into the mug of draft. Tilting his head back, my longtime friend drained the contents in a series of long, slow gulps. After slamming the mug back down on the bar, he wiped his sleeve across the red stubble that had spread across his face over the last few days.

Earlier in the afternoon, Rusty's wife had invited Bailey and me to their apartment for dinner. Jeanne had served grouse that her husband had harvested the previous fall. Seated around their kitchen table, we watched Rusty drain one longneck after another while we talked about the tough times that had descended upon the region. Unable to remember a time when Rusty had drank more than a single beer with his meal, I wasn't surprised when Jeanne took me aside and asked if I'd speak with him.

For a time after 9/11, people feared air flight, canceling their plane reservations, and with northern New England only a car ride away, many outdoor-minded vacationers along the East Coast looked north for their recreation. Guides throughout western Maine saw an increase in the number of sports who booked trips, while local businesses benefited from the increase in traffic. Those coming to the region found the mountains and lakes to their liking, many returning during the following six years, booking rooms in bed-and-breakfasts, motels and cabins, some purchasing a second home.

As sudden and unexpected as the terrorist attack on Lower Manhattan's Trade Center, the economic downturn that began in 2008 caught us all by surprise, affecting even the wealthiest vacationer. As if overnight, the streets of our little town had turned empty, times tougher than any of us could remember. Bookings for guides fell below pre-9/11 numbers while the owners of cabins built along the shores of the lakes were no longer willing to hire a local man to add a room or lay a new roof. Forced to cut back on expenses, those who'd previously paid to have their camps opened and closed now did so themselves. Hell, it seemed like every other cottage had a FOR SALE sign jammed into the front yard.

"Notdistime." Rusty slurred his words. "Some jerk at the bank, a young prick I never saw before, says we got thirty days to bring our payment current." He motioned to Betty for a refill. "If not, they're gon' foreclose."

After completing two tours of duty, the Vietnam veteran had returned to the town where he was born and married Jeanne Reynolds, who was raised in Rangeley, the slightly larger town up the road. The ceremony was performed at Our Lady of the Lakes, the tiny church an easy walk from their apartment located over Lakeview Sports, the sporting goods store that the young couple purchased the following year. Across the street from Ollie Stubbs' general store and just up the block from the bookstore that Bailey would later open, the Millers raised a son while earning enough money to send the boy to a college in Colorado, where he later found employment as a biologist with the Park Service.

Lakeview Sports has stood on the shore of Hawley Pond since it was built in the nineteen fifties, located a short distance from the stone bridge that marks the entrance to the town of Easie and a few steps from the Hawley River. One can hear the stream from the porch where I sometimes sit, staring down into the tannin-stained current, its native brook trout keeping me close, even after all these years.

Although I wasn't around when Rusty returned from Vietnam, those who watched him swim through an ocean of Jack Daniel's, guys like Ollie Stubbs and Merle Lansing, say that if it wasn't for Jeanne, he'd have drowned. It was upsetting to watch him return to those dark waters.

"I said, I'll have another," Rusty shouted to Betty, who had remained at the other end of the bar where the Sox fans were hooting loudly as A-Rod swung through a pitch. When Rusty banged the mug down, one of them glared in our direction.

"What?" Rusty stared down the man, who thought better of a confrontation with the older guide.

After the Yankees' third baseman struck out, the camera panned over the House built by George Steinbrenner, a stadium where neither Rusty nor I could afford a decent seat.

It took the Boston pitcher another fifteen minutes to end the game, the gaggle of guys pulling bills from their jeans and settling up with Betty. Not long afterward, we listened to their expensive vehicles churn up gravel as they patched out of the lot onto the dirt road that forms the main street of town. By now, I'd hoped to be under the covers, lying beside Bailey, feeling the warmth of her thighs against mine. Instead, my skinny white ass ached from sitting on a stool for nearly three hours.

Sometime during the post-game show Rusty had lowered his head onto his arms. Watching Betty clear off the empty bottles and dirty glasses, I suddenly felt trapped inside the lyrics of a Tom Waits song. When she walked back out of the kitchen, I limped down to the other end of the bar and grabbed the broom from her hands.

Chapter Two

I had leaned the broom against the wall and was walking toward the men's room when the roadhouse door swung open. Arthur Wentworth strolled inside hand in hand with Raisa MacDougall, middle daughter of Finley and Beldora. Behind Arthur and Raisa strode Whitney Parker with his wife of only a few years, Raisa's older sister, Sophia. Whit was wearing his deputy's uniform under a yellow rain slicker that fell to his ankles, and when he tipped his cap in my direction, I nodded in reply. As Betty walked toward them, the two couples slid into chairs around a table a few feet from the bar.

"What can I get for you kids?" Weariness had crept into her voice.

By the time I returned from the men's room, the two couples were drinking beer, the guys from bottles, the girls from glasses, as they looked up at the flat-screen T.V., where David Letterman was concluding his monologue.

A few years earlier, like Paul on the road to Damascus, the older of the two Wentworth brothers had seen the light, but it was a fist to the head rather than a bolt from heaven that set the former hooligan straight. After receiving a well-deserved beating at the hands of a former member of the Army's Special Forces, whose skills ranged from carrying out dark ops to creating exquisite floral arrangements, Art and his younger brother, Alvin, now lived behind the flower shop deeded to them by the same man who had knocked sense into the two boys.

While Arthur and Alvin Wentworth were struggling to find salvation,

Raisa MacDougall was choking on the desert dust of Afghanistan, where she spent an extended tour of duty with her National Guard unit, transferring to Iraq before returning home only a few months earlier. Although it appeared that the veteran and the former skinhead had little in common, I was the last to question why a woman chose to love a man.

"You ready to go?" I had resumed my seat beside Rusty, who raised his head and was running his fingers through a thick mop of disheveled red hair. Before he could answer, the late-night host concluded his remarks by announcing that my daughter was to be among his guests for that evening.

Arthur and Raisa immediately rose from their table and pressed in on one side of me while Whitney and his wife did the same on the other.

An hour later, rather than lying warm and comfortable beside Bailey, I found myself still seated at the bar, with Letterman's late-night program drawing to a close. After a commercial about some Star Trek-like device that appeared to do everything except beam its purchaser up to the Enterprise, my daughter walked onto the set, where she took her seat between the *Late Show*'s host and a British movie star. Dressed in a shiny suit and thin tie, his hair greased back on his head, the actor reminded me of a lizard I once saw in the desert outside Las Vegas. I expected his tongue to dart out each time he spoke.

My leg ached more than usual and the pain in my lower back was acting up. Behind me, other residents of the little town had appeared, texted by the two young couples, whose thumbs had not stopped tapping across the keys of their smartphones since hearing the talk show host announce my daughter's name at the beginning of the program.

"I never realized that living in the woods could be so much fun." Letterman smiled into the camera as the studio audience chuckled.

I hadn't seen Prudence since January, when she left to promote the book. On screen, her hair curled down over her shoulders like a series of swollen riffles after a rainstorm. Wearing a short black dress, black heels and sheer stockings, she looked more mature than I remembered.

"For me it's a story about the resiliency of people living in small towns across America," Prudence replied.

"You go, girl," Sophia shouted.

Whitney looked at me from over Rusty's shoulder, but when I looked back, he turned his face away. Like Raisa MacDougall, the young deputy was also a veteran of the Afghanistan war, abandoning his position as the youngest of Rangeley's three-and-a-half-man police force and enlisting in the Marines days after 9/11. But unlike Raisa, Whit had spent time at Walter Reed before returning to friends and family.

"Some people say that the lead character in your novels is based upon your father." The talk show host raised a copy of the book I had written forty years earlier.

"For those of you who don't know, Prudence's father was an icon to those of us growing up in the seventies."

I could see the gap in the talk show host's teeth when he turned from my daughter to the camera.

Rusty, who had been staring at the wet ring left by the bottom of his mug, raised an eyebrow in my direction. He knew about the novel I'd written under the pen name Stephen Rocco, but most everyone else around town had either forgotten about my past or simply knew me as a fishing guide.

"Not really, Dave. The characters in my book are composites of people I've known, combined with those from my imagination."

"But your father does live in the town depicted in your novel?"

I hissed a curse as the talk show host tapped the eraser tip of a pencil against the top of his desk.

My daughter looked uncomfortable, hesitating for a moment before answering yes to the question.

"Well, before we say goodnight for the evening, I understand you have an announcement to make."

Turning from Letterman, my daughter stared into the camera.

"I'm pleased to announce that Lions Gate Films will be making a movie based upon my two books. Filming should begin sometime this summer."

The small gathering that crowded around the television above the bar broke into applause. Ollie Stubbs, sleep still in his eyes, clapped me on the shoulder, Merle Lansing shaking my hand.

Rusty, who had remained seated beside me, pushed his mug toward Betty Leonard and muttered, "I'll have another." Pointing to me, he said, "And pour one for the icon."

Chapter Three

"Robert Dumont?" I frowned at Sam Treadwell, who was reading from an article on the first page of *The Berlin Reporter* while pointing to a photograph of my daughter.

"It says here that the studio is close to signing a deal with him." The veterinarian leaned back, his legs stretched forward, ankles crossed. The soles of his sneakers nearly touched the Jøtul stove, which, like a woodchuck on its hindquarters, squatted across from where he and I sat, our butts comfortably sunk deep into the cushions of two easy chairs as we sipped from our mugs of tea.

Sam wore green scrubs and a dark blue baseball cap, one with a Boston Red Sox logo stitched on the front. Removing the cap, he slid his long fingers through the curly brown hair that fell around his ears and over his brow.

"I think he's perfect to play the mysterious Salvatore D'Amico," he intoned, putting on an announcer's deep voice while readjusting the hat on his head.

It was the week after my daughter's announcement and word had spread quickly through town, everyone excited about the movie, hoping it would revive the local economy, maybe even put the place on the map; everyone except for me. I guess you could say I don't do change very well.

Sam pointed to a second photo, this one of me standing beside a sport, a young guy who grinned up at the camera from beside a stream where he held a large brook trout in his hands. I set down my tea, its color as dark as my mood, its temperature as tepid as my feeling about the impending loss of privacy that was likely to follow when filming began in our small town.

"Robert Dumont?" I repeated, stepping over Rose and grabbing a log from the pile beside the woodstove. The yellow Labrador momentarily lifted her head as I closed the Jøtul's door and sat back across from Sam.

During a long and distinguished career, Dumont had become a well-known actor. Starting in the seventies with his now-famous role as a New York City police detective, he later played characters as diverse as a country-western singer, Catholic priest and Cuban spy.

Rose's tail thumped the floor as Bailey walked around the bookstore's counter. "I think Sal's much more handsome than Robert Dumont."

Flopping into my lap, she swung her legs over the arm of the chair and locked her fingers around my neck. "But I suppose Mr. Dumont will have to do."

Bailey wore jeans and a light blue cotton sweater. A blue ribbon held back auburn hair that brushed against my cheek. She was younger than me, and from time to time I wondered why she hadn't chosen Sam, whom she briefly dated upon first coming to town. Then again, I've always been better at predicting the behavior of fish than that of women. Besides, it was my lap she was sitting on, and as she lowered her head to my shoulder, I cast the thought aside, breathing in the familiar scent of her shampoo.

"I don't know about handsome, but Dumont certainly has as many wrinkles as Sal. Did you see him in that last movie, the one about the retired assassin?"

"But that's what makes Sal look so distinguished." Bailey winked at the veterinarian.

"Well, they're gonna have to get Julia Roberts if they want to do you justice." Sam looked at me and asked, "What do you think?"

When I ignored his question, he said, "They can always dye Gwyneth

Paltrow's hair."

"Don't you have anything better to do?" I twisted out from under Bailey.

"Come to think of it"—Sam glanced at his watch—"I have a surgery scheduled for eleven."

Unfolding his frame from the chair, the lanky vet swallowed the remainder of his tea, then leaned over and kissed Bailey on the cheek. We watched him amble out of the bookstore's open door carrying the caramel-colored mug he had brought in with him twenty minutes earlier.

"I think Timothy Olyphant would be perfect to play Sam." Shifting her hips, Bailey adjusted her position on the chair. She reminded me of a big cat.

"Who?"

"That good-looking actor. You know. He was in that western series you liked to watch on HBO. I'm not quite sure if it's the shape of his bun or the way it moves, but Sam certainly looks like him from behind."

When I didn't answer, she asked, "Don't you think?"

"Jeez-a-wee, girl," I groaned. "I've never considered either man's ass."

"You do know you're my man?" Bailey rose from the chair, folding her arms around my waist.

Before I could answer, she teetered forward, raising her hands toward my shoulders to maintain her balance.

"Hey, kiddo, you okay?" I held her while she steadied her legs.

"Just a bit dizzy. Shoulda eaten something for breakfast." She let out a shaky laugh.

Bailey broke free from my grasp when I attempted to draw her closer. "Oh no you don't," she chuckled, pointing toward a woman who strolled through the door accompanied by two six- or seven-somethings.

The children scrambled toward the back of the store where toys and board games were displayed as their mother stopped to turn a metal carousel containing postcards. While Bailey exchanged pleasantries with her customer, I pulled out the recent issue of the *Northwoods Sporting Journal* from a rack beside the door.

After a while the mom gathered up her kids, and like a mallard, waddled out the door without making a purchase, her two ducklings following behind in single file.

I could see why people in town were looking forward to the making of the movie and the resulting business it would bring, but that didn't mean I had to like it.

Bailey walked around the counter and into her office, coming back out with a large carton. Although I would have preferred to take a nap in front of the stove, there was wood to split and the roof of a lean-to to patch. Replacing the paper in the rack, I pulled on my coat, the short one with the faded green plaid squares, and walked over to the shelf where Bailey was removing books from the box. After kissing her goodbye, I walked toward the door, but turned when she let out a low whistle.

Looking back, I saw that she was pointing at my butt.

"Not bad, mister," she called.

"For an old man, you mean."

"For *my* old man," she countered.

"Ashley Judd," I said.

She looked puzzled.

"Ashley Judd. That's who should play you."

Buttoning the wool coat, I flipped up the collar before sinking my hands into its pockets. Lakeview Sports was only a short walk up the street, but I was happy when I closed the door behind me, the sting from the wind coming off Hawley Pond still biting at my face. I waved to Jeanne, who sat behind the counter, and hobbled down the middle aisle toward the back of the store where Rusty's office was located. A layer of dust had collected on the shelves that contained merchandise from the previous year. Opening the door, I found Buck lying where I'd left him, curled up on a rug.

"C'mon, bub," I whispered.

The old Labrador opened one eye as I gently stroked his side. For many years now, gray fur had advanced over the big dog's black coat. Like the season's first snow, it spread down his chin and along his jowls, around his nose and over his paws. But it was a jagged line where fur had failed to return that made people look twice. I felt responsible for the scar stitched down the left side of his head that made him look like a character from a Tim Burton film.

A few years back I had discovered a dredging operation on the headwaters of the Cupsuptic River, a pristine stretch of water that serves as a natural hatchery for the wild brook trout of our region. With the authorities tripping over their bureaucratic red tape, the dredgers turned their attention to the stream that slips out of the pond beside my cabin. That's when I decided to take matters into my own hands. With the help of the same gentle giant who had straightened out the Wentworth brothers, I destroyed the expensive equipment used to rape the little brooks. A few weeks later the ringleader retaliated by sinking my boat, bashing in Buck's head when the old dog attempted to intervene. It was touch-and-go for a few days, but Sam saved his life, the long jagged scar a reminder of how every action results in a reaction, a law of physics that we so often forget.

Buck slowly rose to his feet, wobbling back down the aisle of the store on legs still unsteady from a morning spent sleeping in the Millers' backroom.

"Things any better?" I asked Jeanne.

Looking up from the counter, she said, "He's been out every night this week. I don't know what I'm going to do, Sal. Haven't seen him like this since he came back from the war."

"Any chance you can work things out with the bank?"

"Rusty told the loan officer that we'd bring our payment current by the end of the summer, but he wants it by the end of this month. Even if we get an extension, I'm not so sure business will pick up the way it usually does once the fishing season starts."

"Where is he?" I asked.

"Out back."

"Mind if I leave Buck with you a while longer? No sense the two of us freezing."

"Sure." Jeanne smiled down while the dog walked around the counter, collapsing beside her chair as if he understood our conversation.

Outside, the wind continued to blow, the clouds sweeping past the sun as I hurried around the back of the store.

"Shut the damn door," Rusty grumbled. His eyes were bloodshot, face unshaven, hair unkempt.

I did as he ordered, rubbing my hands in front of an old cast iron stove that the two of us had pulled out of the Rangeley dump and dragged into the far corner of the guide's work shed. No longer airtight, it worked hard keeping the cold out of the drafty building. Rusty's Rangeley boat lay upside down on a set of blocks in the middle of the room. The guide had scraped and sanded the hull and was now applying a coat of fresh paint.

I walked past the shavings that littered the floor and looked down at the gunmetal-gray paint that glistened under the dull light cast by an overhead bulb. "Some things never change," I said.

The traditional craft handed down from father to son was as sound as it had been when first built in the nineteen forties.

Rusty leaned over and grabbed an open bottle of beer from among the tools scattered between boxes of nails and cans of screws on a table set along the back wall.

"Yeah well, others do," he grunted, after draining the longneck in one long pull.

Chapter Four

Another week had passed since my daughter made her announcement on late-night television. Two days earlier, the ice on Otter Pond had moaned and then groaned, breaking into large pieces sooner than most years. During the next few days, the big lakes would follow.

Standing on the porch of my cabin, I glassed the far shoreline of the pond where the branches of the hardwood trees remained bare. I had spent the week performing the chores required to maintain a fishing camp in the Maine woods. A few days back, I brushed away the cobwebs, sweeping out dog hair left over from the previous year that gathered like little black tumbleweed in every corner of the cabin. After airing out the rooms, I lit the propane stove and refrigerator, checked the gaslights, cleaned the chimney and stocked the kitchen shelves with staples and the wood box with cordwood. The following day, I changed the oil in the generator, filling the tank with fresh gasoline and brushing clean the spark plug before starting it up. I also cleaned the foot valve at the end of a PVC pipe and anchored it in the pond, then primed the pump and filled the cistern behind my cabin with water. Yesterday, I soldered a leaking pipe, spending the remainder of the afternoon patching a persistent leak in the roof over the kitchen.

Perched on a rafter in one corner of the porch, Rocky twittered his approval at being back at the cabin. Having spent the winter confined to Bailey's mudroom, the flying squirrel climbed up a screen window, happy to be on the porch, where he'd spend his nights now that I'd opened the camp for another season.

Hanging the binoculars on a spruce notch, I sat in one of two rockers that faced the pond. A long-handled net and a number of rod tubes leaned on a little green table between the rockers. On the table lay a few reels and small plastic boxes of varying sizes that contained a lifetime of trout and salmon flies.

Officially, Maine's fishing season begins on April 1st, but anyone traveling to our region on that day will find the lakes and ponds under ice, the water temperature on the few rivers that are open close to freezing. Although trout throughout the Middle Atlantic states up through southern New England rise to spring mayfly hatches as early as March, those of us living in western Maine must wait until late May for the first mayflies to trigger fish into looking toward the surface.

Nevertheless, my season as a fishing guide begins as soon as the lakes break free of ice. That's when the salmon and brook trout follow the smelt up the rivers and streams. Within the next few days my sports would be casting their Grey Ghosts and Marabou Muddlers to wild fish willing to strike at anything resembling smelt, the region's principal baitfish. If I did my job, an angler might feel the power of a four-pound salmon or a brook trout measuring twenty or more inches.

It would take most of the afternoon to lube the reels, clean the lines, and check the net and rods for dings, but first I'd go through the flies, starting with my streamers, removing those that were no longer serviceable and making notes as to how many more I'd need to tie.

Like many of the guides, my bookings were down, but on my open dates I knew Grant's Camps on Big Kennebago Lake would throw me some work, as would Tom Rider and Maureen Carter, Tom owning Beaver Den Camps, located at the confluence of the Big and Little Magalloway Rivers on Aziscohos Lake, and Maureen, Lakewood Camps on the Rapid River across from Middle

Dam. All three sporting lodges employed my services whenever one of their young guides called in sick after a weekend bender or for more serious reasons, such as a chainsaw accident or broken heart, two of the more common injuries known to plague young men in western Maine.

A low rumbling sound drew my attention away from the pond. Lying curled in one corner of the porch, Buck had his head tucked under a shoulder, the dog's snores emanating from under his salt-and-pepper fur.

"Whadaya think?" I asked, setting aside a box containing flies meant to imitate Blue-winged Olives, a mayfly that hatches on dark and rainy afternoons throughout the season. Rising from the rocker, I looked down at the old dog.

"How bout we play hooky? An hour on the water, just you and me and those brook trout out there?"

Buck didn't stir, but hearing my voice, Rocky swung down from the porch's ceiling and climbed upon my shoulder. I reached beside the rocker and unscrewed the cap on a jar containing cracked corn while the flying squirrel purred into my ear.

A number of years back I'd retrieved a birdhouse that had fallen to the ground. Unaware that a family of flying squirrels had been living inside, I set it on the porch. By the time Buck heard their cries, the babies inside were too weak to survive, all except Rocky, whom I nursed to health with the help of a formula cooked up by Sam Treadwell.

Setting the squirrel on the table, I grabbed a mug from among the fly boxes and raised it to my lips. My morning tea had grown cold.

I was wearing moccasins over bare feet, a flannel bathrobe over sweatpants and a sweatshirt with the faded outline of a brook trout drawn across the front. The words GOT TROUT? were inscribed on the back. The dark sky was turning slowly blue as the sun struggled to crest the summit of Green Top Mountain, and although the day promised to warm up, according to the thermometer the temperature remained in the high thirties, not atypical for the early part of May.

I rose from the table and adjusted the cloth belt around my waist. Trudging into the kitchen, I pulled up the robe's collar while the squirrel, having climbed into a pocket, nestled inside. Never a fan of tepid tea, I poured the contents into the sink and lit the flame under the red-speckled pot that can always be found on the back burner of my stove.

After a second mug, I walked up to my bedroom and lowered Rocky onto the closet shelf where he spends his daylight hours sleeping in a wooden bird box. Changing into jeans, I buttoned a flannel shirt over a long-sleeve tee and added a fleece pullover before walking back down to the screened-in porch.

"C'mon, old thing." I gently nudged the big dog with the tip of my boot.

The Labrador stared up through eyes still clouded with sleep. I wondered if he dreamed, and if so, what about. Bending to one knee, I slid my hand over his coat. Bumps of varying sizes and shapes had developed across his body. Although Sam called them sebaceous cysts, something, he said, that should not give me concern, I couldn't help but worry.

Unlike humans, whose lives are worn down by fear and regret, dogs don't think about what went before or might lie ahead. As far as I knew, Buck wasted no time thinking about illness or death and had no memories of when we were strong enough to swim across the pond and back, fish from dawn to dark or spend entire days together afield. At least, I didn't think he did. The old dog might feel his age, but unlike me, it didn't appear to bother him. He'd make a perfect Buddhist.

It had been a few years since Buck had lifted a leg to pee, so I waited as he squatted beside a patch of wild blueberry bushes. Afterward, we ambled down the path that led to the pond, stopping beside an immense white pine that stood like a sentry at the end of the short trail. One of the King's trees, it was saved from the loggers' ax prior to the Revolution for future use as a mast on one of His Majesty's ships of the line. For reasons unknown, it was left standing by subsequent loggers, the tree's branches tapering upward for well over one hundred feet, its lower limbs extending outward at least ten feet from around the trunk. The pine tree's bark was thickly encrusted with sap. Across from the massive conifer, on the other side of the path, stood the large flat boulder where my meditations often turn into naps.

Pulling a canoe from under the tree, I wiped away the spiderwebs, twigs and other debris that had collected over the winter months. After doing the same to a smaller canoe, I dragged one after the other down to the edge of the pond. With Buck nestled in the bow of the shorter craft, I stored my gear in the stern and pushed off with a paddle.

My cabin is the only man-made structure on the two-hundred-and-twenty-acre natural impoundment, a tiny opening in a forest that stretches over three hundred thousand acres across western Maine and into northeast New Hampshire, the latter's border an invisible line zigzagging along the far side of the little pond.

To the north and east lay the big lakes. Aziscohos, long, narrow and relatively shallow, follows the original streamed of the Magalloway River down from Camp Ten Bridge to the concrete dam above Route 16, the two-lane road that connects the little towns of Rangeley and Easie with those across the New Hampshire border. Along this fifteen-and-a-half-mile stretch of blacktop lies the two Richardsons joined one to the other by a relatively thin channel called The Narrows, with Upper Dam separating the two vast expanses of water from Mooselookmeguntic Lake, the latter so wide that its northern arm is called Cupsuptic Lake. Below Lower Richardson, falling out of Middle Dam is the Rapid River, the Northeast's premier brook trout tailwater. Farther east, Rangeley Lake accounts for some of the region's largest landlocked salmon, the Rangeley River slipping out from the lake's southwest shoreline and down into Hawley Pond, beside which the town of Easie was founded after the conclusion of the Civil War.

Although not as large, Parmachenee and the Kennebagos, big and small, are set into the northern fringe of the forest like three jewels in a balsam crown, while to the south, stretching back into New Hampshire and fed by the Rapid and Magalloway Rivers, ripple the wild waters of Umbagog Lake. With all this water surrounded by pristine forest, is it any wonder that the region became known as The Land of Fishing Legends?

As I paddled out into the pond, my mind turned to western Maine's fishery. The entire watershed begins with tiny streams that slip across the Canadian border. Connecting the big lakes, one to another, are larger, brawling rivers regulated by dams built in years past to tame their turbulent rapids so as to carry logs down through the surrounding forest, these rivers eventually merging with the biggest of them all, the mighty Androscoggin.

I tied a Mickey Finn to my line and cast toward shore. Trying to picture the small steamer ships that hauled islands of pulpwood across the lakes, I let the red-and-yellow streamer sink under the surface. Stripping it back toward the canoe, I imagined the rivers choked with timber, the sound of dynamite blasting apart logjams. Although it must have been a colorful time, I was thankful that the last river drive occurred sometime in the early sixties, abandoned in favor of trucks that roll over the dirt roads, which have spread through the spruce-and-balsam hills like a river spider's web, returning the water to its former pristine condition where trout and salmon can once again grow large, and men and women like myself can earn a living guiding the sports who seek out these wild fish.

Paddling around the southeast edge of the pond, I cast the streamer toward an old wooden dam that marks the outlet of Otter Brook. Water sweeps through the dam's logs that have fallen into disrepair and around its stone cribwork, forming the little brook that is within easy walking distance of my cabin. Sliding over cobble and stone, the thin ribbon of water slips down through the forest and empties into a hidden cove on the western shore of Aziscohos Lake. I cast again, this time slowly hand-twisting the line back toward the canoe.

In the early part of the nineteenth century a concrete dam was built across the Magalloway River, creating thirteen-mile Aziscohos Lake. Tom Rider maintains his sporting lodge at the head of the lake, the original camp built before the construction of the dam that created the long and narrow body of water. Today, cold water pours from the bottom of the dam, creating a tailwater fishery that can be fished throughout the summer from just above Route 16, more than a mile downstream.

I reeled in. Paddling along the far side of the pond, I came upon a loon newly returned from the ocean, where it had spent the winter. I watched as the large bird preened its black-and-white feathers. The forest descended to the water, the evergreen limbs of spruce and balsam interspersed among the still naked branches of the deciduous trees, mostly birch and aspen, with a lesser amount of maple and oak. Flying along the edge of the pond, a kingfisher chattered its displeasure at my presence.

I snipped off the colorful streamer and replaced it with another, this one called a Black Ghost.

Although not thrilled with the prospect of a bunch of Hollywood types descending upon my tiny bit of the planet, I knew that making a movie would bring badly needed jobs to the town and might regenerate the local economy. I hoped it would pull the Millers out of their financial hole and Rusty from his alcohol-fueled funk, but like a dog eager for his supper, another thought continued to nag at me.

It had been more than forty years since I scorched my feathers flying too close to the sun. Landing beside this tannin-stained pond, I had managed to reinvent myself, shedding the skin of counterculture writer and settling into the routine of fishing guide. Since first hearing my name mentioned on network television, I knew that after all this time, and despite my best efforts to the contrary, Stephen Rocco was about to catch up with Salvatore D'Amico.

While Buck slept in the bow of the canoe, I paddled between the shoreline and a small spit of land. I cast between the island's partially submerged bushes, the pond swollen with snow melt and spring rain. In the coming weeks, the water level would gradually recede, soon to reveal patches of wild iris.

I looked forward to August, a pleasant time of year when the bugs cease their bloodthirsty attacks and most sports return home, having had their fill of the big trout that typify spring fishing. It's a time when Bailey and I can pull the canoe onto the island's natural beach of fine grit, spread out a towel, and bake our tired bones under the summer sun.

Working my way across the pond, I pulled back on the rod as a sudden boil engulfed the little streamer. My pulse quickened when a brookie rolled, its crimson side flashing in the early morning sunlight. Moments later, I held the first trout of the new season, its flank glistening as the fish slipped from my moistened palm.

Chapter Five

After spending a pleasant morning on the pond, I convinced myself that there was no reason for worry; after all, who would care about a one-book wonder who hadn't been heard from since the nineteen seventies? Buck had padded into the wood while I fixed a lunch of chicken simmered in a white wine sauce with garlic, onions and boiled potatoes left over from the previous evening.

Later that afternoon, I found myself bumping over potholes that had developed during the freeze and thaw of the last few months. With the truck's radio always on the fritz, I cranked up the aftermarket CD player Junior Ross had installed for me during the winter. Buck had his nose out the window and his ears flopping backward, as he enjoyed the scents of the new season. Over the rush of sweet air, Steve Earle sang of love lost while I told myself that no one was going to bother with an aging writer.

Stopping once to watch a doe cross the road and again to navigate over a partially blown-out culvert, I came to the blacktop. As an SUV with Connecticut plates sped past, I noticed that the sign for the Morton Cutoff Road had been removed. For as long as I could remember, the wooden marker had been nailed to a tree beside Route 16 to designate the major logging road connecting the blacktop with the network of dirt-and-gravel roads and two-tracks that fanned out into the forest.

Ten minutes later I pulled beside Bailey's bookstore, where a number of people were milling outside the door. Happy to see business picking up, I walked around to the passenger side of the Toyota to help the old dog down onto the gravel. As I did, a man pointed in my direction, the others in the group following him toward my truck.

As they drew closer, I could see that there were five of them, three men and two women, all young, none over thirty. One of the women, the first to reach me, raised a copy of *Desperadoes of the Mind*, and asked if I'd sign it. The others soon gathered around, each holding out a copy of the book I'd written during what seemed like a lifetime ago. I tried not to show my displeasure, and borrowing a pen from one of the men, scratched my name across the title page, handing the book back to the woman.

"Salvatore Da, Dam me, co?" She had trouble pronouncing my last name.

"Yes?" I asked while she stared down at my signature.

"But I thought your name was Stephen Rocco?"

"His pen name." The man who lent me the ballpoint corrected her with a frown.

I was wondering how they recognized me when the other woman in the group, a ring in her nose and a sleeve of tattoos adorning each of her arms, raised a book for me to sign. The covey of young men and women parted when Buck suddenly squatted, an unsteady stream of urine dribbling down his leg and forming a tiny brooklet that ended in a small puddle between them.

I found the answer inside the store. Bailey had pasted a newspaper article onto a large poster board and set it on a table that contained a number of my books displayed between stacks of my daughter's newest novel. The article contained photos of Prudence and of me, one taken from the inside cover of my book, the artist as a young man, and the other, a more recent photograph of the grizzled guide beside his smiling sport, the latter cradling an exceptionally large salmon in his hands.

Comparing *Desperadoes of the Mind* with my daughter's two books, the article began:

> Like J.D. Salinger before him, counterculture author Salvatore D'Amico, aka Stephen Rocco, vanished from the limelight after writing a novel that captured the imagination of a generation. Since his wife, a rock legend, died of a drug overdose, little has been known of the writer's whereabouts.
>
> With the making of a movie based upon his daughter's novels, D'Amico, who has been living in the small town of Easie, located in western Maine, has been rediscovered by a new generation of readers eager to make his acquaintance. The movie, to be made on location, will be directed by Bruno Magalini.

"Jeez-a-wee!" I stared at Bailey in disbelief.

"I know, sweetie, but the phone started to ring after Pru's appearance on *Letterman*, really going nuts after the *New York Times* article came out." She pointed to the table and then nodded toward the five young people outside the store. "Those kids drove all the way up from Boston hoping to meet you."

"You're the man." Richard Morrell was making himself a mug of coffee. Black hair fell loosely down the back of his leather jacket. His work pants were stained with oil and pitch.

"*Et tu?*" I pulled a mug from the rack on the counter, and after making myself a cup of tea, flopped down in the easy chair across from the Jøtul stove.

"Gotta learn to ride the wave." Morrell sank into the chair next to mine.

A moment later Rose appeared, bouncing happily out of Bailey's office to nuzzle Buck's face. Lowering a hand to stroke Rose's coat, the Native American raised his mug of coffee with the other. Bailey started in our direction, but then turned after a couple entered the store. When they stopped at the table beside the door, she looked back over her shoulder and said, "It's been like this all week."

"I swear these dogs have more sense." I stared down at the two Labs, who had settled down around our feet.

"Word," Morrell mumbled.

The Wabanaki had attended the Rangeley Lakes Regional High School with Rusty Miller, the two of them enlisting in the Army, both serving two tours in Vietnam. But unlike Rusty, his friend settled on the West Coast, the men quickly renewing their friendship when Morrell unexpectedly returned to his home after more than forty years.

"You resolve your differences with Baybrook?" I asked.

The summer after his return, Richard Morrell had built himself a cabin along the eastern shore of Parmachenee Lake. Although the Wabanaki claimed ownership of the land by virtue of his Native American heritage, the company that held the deed commenced proceedings to have him evicted.

According to Rusty, Morrell hadn't made much of his Wabanaki heritage before enlisting in the Army. It was while living on the west coast that the Native American traced his lineage back to Chief Metallak, a locally known historical character, who, it was said, had lived for one hundred and twenty years. Metallak was reputed to have moved his tribe from the Magalloway Valley to the St. Francis River in Canada, returning to the wilderness surrounding the lake named for his daughter sometime after Roger's Rangers crossed over the border to prosecute America's part in England's one-hundred-year war with the French.

The Native American argued that he didn't need a white man's deed for property originally owned by his family, a position that successfully resisted the paper company's initial legal assault. With the ultimate outcome far from certain, the Wabanaki had declared his willingness to sign over all rights to the Parmachenee tract in exchange for the few acres around his cabin.

"Looks like they're not interested in settling, which is fine with me. They win, I move. I win, they lose all the land surrounding my family's lake and maybe the entire valley."

Rusty once told me that while in basic training Morrell had won a pot of more than ten thousand dollars with only a pair of threes.

"Did you know that the sign for the Morton Cutoff Road is down?" I asked him.

"Hadn't noticed." The Wabanaki took another sip of coffee.

As Bailey rang up another sale, the conversation drifted toward our mutual friend.

"If he doesn't get his head out of the bottle, they're gonna lose the store for sure," I said.

"No doubt," Morrell agreed.

Finishing his coffee, the alleged descendent of Chief Metallak rose from his chair. After returning his mug to the counter, he walked outside, the pinup smiling from the back of his leather jacket.

"Much too tense." Bailey was standing behind me, her fingers digging into my shoulders.

Before I could answer, two men and a woman came into the store. After stopping at the table, one of the guys mumbled something to the others, who nodded their heads in my direction.

I followed Bailey to the counter, handing her my mug. "It appears you have more customers, and I've got to get over to Ollie's if we're gonna eat dinner tonight."

"Did you see all those buses that pulled into the Hawley Inn?"

I was standing in the vegetable aisle of Easie's general store inspecting an eggplant when the owner appeared, his belly splashing down under an apron tied around his expansive waist. Ollie Stubbs was a large man, not quite six feet tall, but built like a fireplug with a face that reminded me of a bulldog. In his eighties, he favored suspenders, the kind that clipped to the top of his jeans. Thanks to his four children and nine grandchildren, Ollie had a variety of pairs, receiving another with each passing holiday. This afternoon's selection bore a number of gaily-colored pheasants flying up and down the bands that stretched over the older man's shoulders.

I slid the eggplant into a plastic bag that already contained a few red and yellow peppers and a couple of sweet onions.

"Can't say as I did," I replied.

"Everybody's been talking about it. They drove past early this morning, one vehicle after another. The whole town came out onto the street to gawk at them. Reminded me of Paris back in forty-four."

"That right?" I picked up a container of mushrooms. "These fresh?" I asked.

"Richard Morrell brought them in this morning. Picked them somewhere up to Parmachenee. Wouldn't tell me exactly where."

I placed the mushrooms in my bag.

"Hawley'll be booked solid until the film's over." A grimace slipped over the portly grocer's features.

Joseph Hawley owned The Hawley Inn, a twenty-four-room facility with a gourmet restaurant, state-of-the-art spa and an Olympic-size swimming pool. The Inn's nineteen-hole golf course overlooked Hawley Pond. The richest man in Franklin County also owned Hawley's Landing. Some of the old-timers still remembered how he built the modern marina on the site of the Easie Fish and Game Club, a sporting club created by his father, after he'd returned from the same war that Ollie fought in, a club opened to every resident of the town. Today, twenty-foot fiberglass skiffs bob gently in their slips where once a fleet of wooden Rangeley boats had been tied along an old wharf, with few, if any, of the town's full-time residents able to afford the exorbitant fees charged by Hawley to vacationers needing a place to dock their boats during the summer.

Ollie had a more personal reason for disliking the younger entrepreneur, who had called in a loan that Hawley's father had previously granted to his wartime buddy at a favorable rate.

Always looking for more, Joseph Hawley divided his time between a brownstone on Boston's Beacon Hill that he inherited from his mother, a Florida condominum in Palm Springs, and the six-thousand-square-foot log home he had built on the pond named after the founder of the town, his great-grandfather, Joshua Hawley.

As Planning Board chairman, Joe Hawley enforced those restrictive land use regulations that advanced his business interests while taking advantage of every development opportunity, however damaging it might be to the surrounding lakes, rivers and streams. It was Hawley who had pushed through the approvals for a development plan that nearly destroyed Otter Pond, and although it might be impossible to prove, I was sure that he had been involved in the illegal dredging of Otter Brook.

There was no love lost between us.

"I hear your book's selling like hotcakes over to Christine's. I'm thinking about ordering a bunch of copies, putting them out next to the register."

I said nothing while working my way down to the fruit bins. "We have a special on bananas," Ollie offered, pointing to a cardboard sign.

Grabbing a bunch, I added them to the vegetables, inspecting the oranges before collecting a dozen from the shelf.

"You hear about Rusty?" he asked in a hushed tone.

I'm usually the last one to hear any gossip, living out on the pond with no phone or Internet service, but figured the news couldn't be good.

"Lester stopped him night before last driving back from Rangeley."

Lester Crocker was chief of the three-and-a-half-man Rangeley police force.

"OUI?"

"Jeanne told my Janet that Rusty was due back for dinner around seven. He had been out all afternoon guiding three guys on Lower Richardson Lake. Took them out in that Rangeley boat of his. According to Jeanne, when they returned, the three sports insisted that Rusty join them for beers over to the Red Onion in Rangeley."

A young couple walked down the aisle, the man staring in my direction, then saying something that made the woman giggle. Ollie waited for them to pass before continuing.

"It was after midnight when Lester stopped him. Left Rusty's truck with the Rangeley still on the trailer by the side of the road and drove him home. Told Jeanne if it happened again, he'd throw the book at him."

"Ollie," Janet Stubbs called from behind the counter, "telephone."

Ollie shrugged his shoulders before lumbering back up the aisle.

After paying for my groceries, I walked out onto the large deck outside the store, where I found Bobby Mendez and three other young men hunched over a picnic table eating a late lunch. All four wore the green uniform of the Border Patrol. Across the table sat Ronnie Adams, the words **GAME WARDEN** stenciled across the back of a long-sleeve T-shirt. Beside Ronnie sat the one-half of Rangeley's three-and-one-half-man police department. Dressed in his blue uniform, Whitney Parker's face was hidden under the shadow cast by the brim of a dark blue baseball cap with the department's insignia stitched on the front. Seated next to him, a deputy wore the brown-and-tan of the Franklin County Sheriff's Office, a Smokey the Bear hat on his knee, his eyes hidden behind mirrored sunglasses.

Lester Crocker leaned against the wall, the visor of his hat high on his head, the setting sun shining down upon his face. With one leg crossed in front of the other, his ample belly pressed against a starched shirt, the chief clamped his thumbs into the belt loops of his pants.

"How's fishin'?" he asked.

"Fair to middling." I gave my usual response to the question most everyone asks a fishing guide.

Leaning in, I spoke in a low voice so the others would not hear. "Want to thank you for what you did for Rusty."

Saying nothing, he stepped around Buck and leaned over Whitney's shoulder.

"You gonna eat that pickle?"

"*Hola, patrón.*" Bobby Mendez looked up between bites of his grinder, Ronnie and Whit nodding in my direction. It seemed to me that a smart criminal might consider this the perfect time to commit a crime, seeing as just about anybody who was somebody in law enforcement was feeding his face on the porch of Ollie's store, but I said nothing.

Buck, who had been waiting outside while I shopped for dinner, sat beside the county deputy, saliva drooling down his jaw as the big dog stared intently at a bit of ham that dangled from between two slices of white bread. When the deputy lowered his sandwich to a paper plate, I watched the big dog draw closer, his muscles rippling with anticipation.

"I'd like to report a crime in progress." I pointed at the sandwich.

The entire table stared down at Buck, but the sheriff's deputy was too slow, the dog lunging at the paper plate, coming away with the sliver of ham and a large chunk of sandwich.

The Smokey the Bear hat fell to the floor when the deputy rose from the bench. His eyes hidden behind mirrored sunglasses, he shifted his head from the disheveled sandwich to the dog and then back to his sandwich while the others, unable to contain their laughter, drew their meals closer.

After swallowing his prize in a single gulp, Buck stood his ground, but trying to avoid any hard feelings, I pulled out a ten-dollar bill and handed it to the guy, shrugging my shoulders as we both looked down at the dog.

"Might as well give him the rest of it," Lester drawled.

As the young man shuffled inside the store, Buck devoured the remainder of the sandwich.

"Speaking of crimes in progress, you know anything about the destruction of signage along the logging roads?" The others around the table looked up as the chief asked me the question.

"I noticed that the Morton Cutoff marker was down."

"It's happening all over." Whitney Parker lowered his face when I looked in his direction.

"Day before yesterday the mile markers on the Tim Pond logging road went missing." Ronnie Adams rose to dump his paper plate into the trash can.

"Same with the signs beside Little Kennebago Pond." This coming from one of the border patrol agents.

"Gashes in the trees where they had been nailed," Whitney said.

"Gashes?"

"Looked like bear. Like they do to mark their territory," he replied.

"Would have to be an awfully smart bear, tearing down paper company signs," Ronnie added.

There is little mystery to crime in a small town. Those working in law enforcement are on a first-name basis with those who make their living off the hard work of others. They may not always be able to prove it, and sometimes may even look the other way, but the list of suspects is usually a short one that rarely changes. So it wasn't a surprise when everyone at the table raised their eyes to watch Arthur Wentworth, Sr. saunter up the street. The father of Arthur, Jr. and Alvin Wentworth plucked a cigarette from the corner of his mouth and flicked it toward the ground as he climbed the steps of the deck. The elder Wentworth's hair fell down either side of his face from under a cap caked with grease and oil. He appeared to have slept in his clothes. His sharp nose fell below eyes like slits that shifted from side to side, reminding me of a fox on the lookout for easy prey.

"Gentlemen." His grin revealed a dental hygienist's nightmare.

"Arthur." The chief took a step back to allow the other man to pass into the store.

Chapter Six

"Jeanne is beside herself," Bailey called from the couch. Now that the food was gone, Buck and Rose lay sprawled at her feet, the older dog on his side, snoring loudly, the younger on her back, legs spread wide.

I had prepared chunks of chicken with the onions, peppers and bits of fried eggplant, adding various herbs, at the last minute mixing in Richard Morrell's wild mushrooms with some noodles to complete the meal. Now, standing at the sink, I set the last dish in the rack while folding a towel over my shoulder. Although Bailey had hardly touched her glass, I thought the red wine had gone well with the meal. Pushing the cork back into the bottle, I placed it on the kitchen counter and padded onto the rug in the adjoining room where Bailey sat watching the evening news.

"Here you go." I stood, my bare feet between the jumble of sleeping dogs, lowering a mug of hot tea to the coaster set out on the maple table in front of the couch. After only a few bites of dinner, Bailey had complained that she was stuffed, slipping out of her shoes and changing from jeans and a sweater into an oversized T-shirt. It was still early in the season and her thighs remained pale between the bottom of the tee and the top of the dark green kneesocks she prefers wearing on cool evenings.

I carried my tea to the glass door that overlooked Hawley Pond. The mug warmed the palms of my hands.

"I've tried my best. I really have." I spoke with my back to her while staring out the door. The large body of water reflected the stars that glittered down from across a galaxy that paid no notice to the concerns of our planet's residents.

"I know you have. I'm as worried for Jeanne as I am for Rusty," she replied.

I raised the mug to my lips and blew across the tea's surface before taking a slow sip. Closing the curtain, I walked across the room. Bailey sighed as I slid beside her. I raised my legs over the dogs, crossing my feet on the table. Grabbing the remote, I turned off the television. Rose looked up for a moment, but then lowered her head against Buck's rump.

"I don't see where they're going to get the money to bring their loan current." Bailey leaned her head on my shoulder.

"How's your store doing?" I asked, knowing that she too had mortgage payments to make.

"Until this week I had my concerns, but if your book keeps selling, what with the business that Pru's movie should bring in, I'll be fine."

"From what Ollie says, it's already helped Hawley. His inn is booked solid." I slipped my fingers through her auburn hair.

"Why is it that Joe Hawley seems to benefit whether from good fortune or bad while the rest of us struggle to sweep up the crumbs?" Bailey took a sip of her tea.

"Trickle-down theory, I guess."

"Trickle being the operative word." Bailey slid her mug back onto the coaster. "Be right back," she called while rising to walk quickly down the hall.

I climbed over the two dogs, their heads raised to see what all the movement was about, and made my way over to a combination radio/CD player that sat atop a narrow cabinet in the far corner of the room. Opening the cabinet door, I sifted through the discs stacked inside until finding one to my liking.

"I hope it wasn't my cooking?" I called toward the bathroom. Sliding the disc into the slot, I returned to the couch, where Buck had already settled back to sleep, and patted Rose on the head before picking up my mug.

I had nearly finished my tea by the time Bailey returned. She looked a bit shaky, but smiling that smile that had captured my heart the first time I saw her. From the corner of the room, the raspy voice of the French-speaking singer rose over the oscillating notes of an accordion.

Bailey pointed to the CD player that I had cranked up.

"Figured a bit of Cajun music might take your mind off your troubles." I rose, about to twirl her in my arms, but she stepped back.

"I think I'd better sit down." Bailey smiled weakly.

I slid down on the couch beside her.

"Dinner was great. Just didn't settle right." She slipped her head down onto my lap, curling her knees up into her chest.

I closed my eyes as the accordion music two-stepped through the small room. When I opened them again, the phone was ringing. My thigh had stiffened up on me, and after slipping out from under Bailey, I limped around the dogs and into the kitchen.

"Salvatore?" It was Jeanne Miller. "Come quick." The phone went dead before I could answer.

I left Bailey snoring fitfully, and after sliding on my socks and boots, hustled the short distance up the street to Lakeview Sports. The night was cool, but not uncomfortable. Turning the corner, I found Joe Hawley sprawled on the ground with Rusty Miller, his fists clenched, standing over him.

"Salvatore!" Jeanne cried from where she stood on the porch.

"Need any help?" I asked.

"Get this lunatic away from me." Joseph Hawley, his arms behind him, butt to the ground, struggled to crawl backwards. He looked every bit the well-dressed crayfish in his tan pants and Docksides.

"I was talking to Rusty," I replied.

Hobbling toward the guide, I whispered, "I'm not sure Lester's gonna cut you a break twice in the same week."

"Hell, that asshole fell down the stairs before I touched him. I haven't even got started."

I looked over at Hawley, who had risen to one knee, his eyes fixed on Rusty while he dusted the grit from the back of his chinos.

"That true, Joe?" I asked.

"You'll be hearing from my lawyers," the wealthiest man in Franklin County screamed.

Backing toward his yellow Humvee, Hawley climbed inside and slammed the door behind him, grit flying everywhere as he pulled onto the street.

Rusty shrugged off the hand I placed on his shoulder, trudging up the steps and past his wife. Jeanne's face was streaked with tears.

"I didn't lay a hand on him," he yelled from inside the store.

Jeanne asked me to come up to their apartment, where we found Rusty seated in the kitchen, an open bottle of whiskey on the table and his twenty-two leaning in the corner by the door. Pulling out a chair, I grabbed the shot glass out of his hand and yelled, "This has gotta stop!"

The guide stared at me through bloodshot eyes, the muscle across his jaw twitching. I had known Rusty for a long time, but wasn't sure what he might do until his shoulders slumped forward.

"Do you believe that guy?" he growled.

I looked at Jeanne, her eyes still wide with terror.

"Hawley stopped by to make us an offer on the store. Said he'd buy out our mortgage. Said if the bank forecloses we'd not only lose the store but everything else we own. At least this way we could keep our savings, maybe start over." Jeanne collapsed into a chair beside her husband. When she lowered her head, I heard sobs from between her folded arms.

"Start over? At our age? Besides, we don't have any damn savings." Rusty drew the fingers of both hands through his red hair.

"Everything we ever made is sunk into the store." Jeanne looked up, her eyes as red as her husband's.

"You should have seen him stutter when I grabbed the twenty-two." Rusty pointed to the rifle that leaned in the corner. "Ran so fast he slipped and fell down the porch steps. The damn thing wasn't even loaded." Rusty let out a nasty laugh. "I figured he wasn't worth the cost of a cartridge."

Chapter Seven

No sooner had I rolled over the stone bridge leading out of town than Buck had fallen asleep. With the window partially open, I could hear the Toyota's engine stammering and stuttering while driving up the Morton Cutoff Road. After turning left onto the Lincoln Pond logging road, I slipped a disc into the CD player and turned up the sound, listening to Ramblin' Jack Elliot sing about Jack Kerouac's Last Dream. I had met the writer while working on my book. It was a number of years after the publication of his celebrated novel, *On the Road*.

The pickup's headlights sliced through the pre-dawn darkness while I thought back to that evening. The man, who against his wishes became the face of the beat generation, was at the end of his career as I was aspiring to begin my own. By that time, a haze of alcohol and drugs had replaced the adrenaline rush that fueled his early years. He had been kind, and I remembered him providing gentle criticism of an early draft of my novel while encouraging me to keep working on it.

After calming Jeanne, I had tried my best to convince Rusty that they'd find a way to bring the loan current if only he'd stop drinking. I wanted to return to the warmth of Bailey's bed, but thought it best to head back to my cabin, having scheduled my first sport of the new season for the following morning. It was well past midnight when I rounded up Buck and left town.

While driving up the Green Top logging road I noticed a dark shroud slipping across the sky. By the time I came down off the mountain road, a light drizzle had begun to fall. With the lights of the Toyota cutting through the mist, I noticed that the sign for the Camp Ten Bridge was no longer on the tree where it had been nailed earlier that morning. Curious, I grabbed a flashlight from the glove box, and with the truck still running, climbed out into the light rain. The flashlight's beam fixed on a set of deep gashes dug into the tree just as Ronnie and Whit had described.

When I first came to the Rangeley Lakes Region there was no signage, except for the Morton Cutoff Road. That was in the late seventies. Back then, they had run out of telephone wire somewhere outside of Easie, leaving those who lived between the outskirts of town and the New Hampshire border without service. It wasn't until the late eighties when Merle Lansing discovered rolls of the stuff in a dark corner of the phone company's warehouse that the line was completed. Only recently had the Brown Company posted signs along its roads, soon thereafter adding mileage markers, with the other paper companies quickly following its lead. In addition to helping crews with their logging operations, the signage also aided law enforcement and emergency services as well as sports searching for some secret honey hole hastily scribbled on a mustard-stained napkin over beers at the Red Onion or the Wooden Nickel.

I climbed back into the truck fairly certain that bears were not systematically removing signs from the logging roads. Trouble was, most old-timers resented the signs, feeling that finding a favorite pool or run should be earned, the signs making it too easy. Any one or more of them could be taking them down, although this didn't account for why bears were marking the same trees where the signs had once been posted. I was too tired to ponder these mysteries for long, fighting to keep my eyes open.

The truck's frayed wipers did little to wick away the rain that began in earnest as I came to the head of Aziscohos Lake and crossed over the Camp Ten Bridge. Rolling down my window, I listened to the Big Magalloway sweep under the planks of the wooden structure. Not far down river, Tom Rider's lodge was lost in the rain that fell with increased intensity.

A few minutes later, I stopped again, this time on the smaller bridge that traverses the Little Magalloway River. Less than a quarter-mile upstream a wide bend in the tannin-stained brook known as Long Pond held trout as long as my arm. The deepest pool on the Little Magalloway, it was a place as dark and moody as Jack Kerouac's restless soul. It would be another few hours before dawn, and I needed some sleep if I was going to be any good to my sport. The plan had been for us to meet at my cabin sometime around six, where I'd fix breakfast while we decided where to fish. I was about to drive off when something on the far bank caught my eye.

For the second time, I stepped out into the cold rain. The flashlight's beam fixed on a white Styrofoam container that stood out against the dark. A few feet away, scattered between their entrails, the light illuminated the heads of at least two dozen pan-sized brook trout, their lifeless eyes staring up at me through the rain.

Climbing back into the warmth of the truck's cab, I pushed down on the gas, crossing under the Fly-Fishing Only sign stapled to the trunk of a large birch tree. A few minutes later, I turned south onto the rutted two-track that leads to my cabin, working my way along the narrow road. A mile or so in, I slowed once again. Tired and wet, I was about to turn down the drive to my cabin when my headlights caught a glint of metal farther down the road. Creeping forward, I came upon a mud-splattered late-model American pickup pulled to one side, a few feet from the culvert through which Otter Brook passes on its way to Aziscohos Lake.

Opening the window, I folded back the Toyota's side-view mirror and slid past the other truck. Freshened by the hard rain, the little brook's current rushed through the culvert, where it disappeared into the blackness of the forest. A few yards up the road I turned around in a small opening once used by loggers as a depot for their lumber and drove back toward the American-made truck. Slipping the Toyota into neutral, I pulled up the emergency brake before climbing outside. I thought I'd seen the truck before, but it was hard to tell in the dark. The lights of the other vehicle were off and the cab vacant.

The truck's rusted tailgate was down, and shining my flashlight into the bed, I saw a number of empty beer cans scattered among a pile of chain and some coils of rope next to a shovel, pickax, and a red plastic gas tank. As I walked toward the cab, a tall man with a wiry frame emerged from the forest. He had the hood of a poncho up around his face and the bill of his cap over his eyes. He held a cigarette between thin lips and when he drew in breath, the end glowed red, momentarily illuminating the creases in his cheeks that ran through a forest of dark stubble. As he drew closer, I recognized his eyes. They were the eyes of a badger.

"Horace," I said, backing up a step.

"Salvatore," he replied, the cigarette dangling from the corner of his mouth. "Didn't know you were back."

"Been home for a week now." Horace Baker looked past me. Pointing toward my truck, where Buck had his nose to the window, he said, "How's that hard-headed dog of yours? Always was a tough sonavabitch."

When Baker raised his left hand to remove the cigarette from his lips, I saw the two stumps that remained after he'd severed his fingers to the knuckles in a chainsaw accident.

Anyone living in the region for even a short period of time could tell you at least one story about Horace Baker, a man, it was said, not to be trifled with, especially alone, in the rain, on a two-track far off the main road. Rumor had it that the fingers had been lost when Horace was only a kid of ten or eleven, ever since then floating in a jar of formaldehyde that he kept on the mantel of his fireplace. He flicked the cigarette onto the ground, grinding it into the rain-soaked dirt with his work boot.

"Back in camp?" I asked him.

"Ahya," he said, leaning against his truck while making no move to open the door.

"Problem?" I looked at the vehicle and then back at the man.

"Nothin' I can't handle," he replied.

Nodding, I tipped the brim of my cap and turned back toward the Toyota. Rain had soaked through my shirt and the damp material began to fog up the cab as soon as I climbed inside. I turned up the defroster before squeezing past the other truck, braking when Horace motioned for me to crank down the window.

"You be sure to tell that young warden I said hello," he drawled. A grin slipped past his thin lips.

Turning down the grassy lane that leads to my camp, I was surprised to find the lights on and smoke swirling up from the cabin's stovepipe into the mist-filled air. My mind was as tired as the old truck. I wondered if I'd actually met the most notorious poacher in two counties or perhaps only imagined it.

After helping Buck out of the truck, I trudged around a mud-splattered minivan with the words "I DIG BONES" emblazoned below a Jolly Roger painted across its sliding door. While I trudged up the stairs and onto the porch, the old dog lumbered over to the lupine garden Bailey had helped me plant. As he squatted, I dropped my rod case and small duffel beside a canvas backpack that leaned against the green table. The pack had a decal stitched along its front similar to the logo I had seen painted across the door of the minivan.

"Hiya." A roly-poly figure threw open the door to the kitchen. Like a herd of wild sheep tramping down a Connemara ravine, a series of unruly curls rolled out from under a sweat-stained Chicago Cubs baseball cap. The blond locks continued their descent around the woman's ears and down her shoulders, framing a face full of freckles. Without benefit of a bra, a mud-stained T-shirt fought a losing battle to control breasts that pressed against the cotton material while the pockets of her baggy cargo pants sagged with the weight of objects unknown.

"You look knackered," she said, turning back into the room.

"Long day." I followed her into the kitchen. "And a longer night," I added, hanging my cap on the rack by the door.

"I'd pour the tea, but you look like you could use a pint." Hollyhock Leventhal was not only my sport; she was also my good friend.

Groaning, I slumped into a chair at the table where I normally take my meals while Holly wobbled toward the refrigerator, her red high-top sneakers shuffling across the kitchen's linoleum floor. Buck, who had nosed open the porch door, dragged himself inside and onto the rug in the adjoining room, the big dog curling under the table where I sat.

Untying the laces of my boots, I kicked them to the side and padded into the living room in my wool socks. I grabbed a few logs from the wood box and added them to the fire Holly had started in the woodstove. After sliding my socks off, I slipped on my fleece moccasins and walked back into the kitchen that was growing pleasantly warm.

Hollyhock had pulled two cans of Guinness from the refrigerator.

"Brought them over special," she said, grabbing two large glasses from inside the cabinet beside the sink.

I watched her pop open a can, pouring the dark stout against the side of the glass and stopping when it was three-quarters full. Foam rose slowly above the rich brown liquid.

My sport was named after the flowers planted outside her mother's home. She had once shown me photographs of the stone structure while recounting the story of how her mother had left the tiny seaside town as a teen, taking a plane from Shannon Airport to Heathrow to study in London. It was while on holiday that Bridget McCue met Ari Leventhal, a private in the Israeli army. Although raised in Tel Aviv, their daughter returned each summer to the western coastline of the Emerald Isle to spend time with her grandmother.

After using the same ritual to pour out the second can of Guinness, Holly bounced back into the kitchen and returned with a round tin.

"When did you get in?" I asked.

"Flew into Rangeley early this morning, picked up my car at Wayne's station and drove in this afternoon. Had my camp set up before dark." She popped open the tin that contained a pile of sugar cookies, each in the shape of a different fish.

"My grand's recipe. I baked them before my flight."

I grabbed a bass and bit off its head.

"You bring Rocky down from the bedroom closet?" I asked.

"Cheeky fellow, that one is. Chattered away until I found that jar of corn you keep on the porch. Little bugger stuffed his face and then climbed onto a rafter without as much as a thank you." Holly chuckled while grabbing a pickerel out of the tin.

"Been here long?" I finished off the bass and started on a perch.

"Walked over sometime after dark. I expected to find you home and decided to wait rather than slog back in the rain." She nibbled on the pickerel's tail.

I liked this woman, whom I had guided over a number of years. Holly raised a glass, inspecting the level of foam that had risen an inch or so, and then set it aside.

Hollyhock Leventhal had been returning to our river valley since 1980, when, as a student, she aided with the excavation of a Paleo-Indian site discovered by Francis Vail along a channel of Aziscohos Lake, which had been drained for repairs on its dam. A local fisherman, Vail had been out searching the exposed bottom for abandoned lures when he found remnants of prehistoric knives and pottery.

Since then, Holly had navigated through the politics of higher education, recently abandoning a position as the head of the paleontology department at a prestigious university to accept the offer of a smaller Midwest college that would allow her to spend more time in the field. Over the last few years she had also jettisoned a husband, returned to her maiden name and acquired an addiction to fly fishing, which is how we met.

My sport once again raised the glass of Guinness, which by then had formed a rich head of foam. She handed it to me after adding the remaining contents of the can. Doing the same with her glass, Hollyhock called out, "Mazel Tov."

Wiping foam from her upper lip, the paleontologist looked toward the ceiling as the rain kept up a steady beat against the cabin's roof.

"Doesn't sound like we'll be going out this mornin'." Pulling a salmon from the tin, she broke off a dorsal fin coated with black and silver sprinkles and plopped it into her mouth.

"How 'bout we try later in the afternoon? Give the storm time to blow through while I get a few hours' sleep." I tried unsuccessfully to stifle a yawn.

When I thought I might lose my cabin to a condominium project, it was Holly who realized that a large bone the dogs had found along the upper portion of Otter Brook belonged not to a moose as we first believed, but rather a mastodon, a discovery that resulted in a site rivaling the one under the lake. The dig saved the land around my cabin from the development scheme cooked up by Joe Hawley. Each spring since then, Holly has set up camp along the bank of the little brook that is only a short walk from my cabin and no more than a half-mile from where Horace Baker had parked his truck alongside the two-track.

"Another?" she asked, draining her glass.

"Why not?" I said, the sound of the rain against the cabin roof not unpleasant.

With her camp so close to my cabin, the paleontologist would drop by whenever she found time, sleeping over in the spare bedroom if the weather

turned especially foul. On nights when the skies were clear of cloud, the two of us would sit under the stars discussing the varied interests we shared, always gravitating back to the subject of fish and the places where they reside. To quote John Voelker, Hollyhock Leventhal shared my love for "the environs where trout are found, which are invariably beautiful," and hated "the environs where crowds of people are found, which are invaribly ugly."

"So, darlin', are we gonna get pissed for no reason or are ya gonna tell me what's been goin' on since last summer?" she asked while we waited for a second set of heads to form in our glasses.

As we munched on cookies, I told the professor of paleontology about the movie, enduring her ribbing at my discomfort over the renewed interest in my book. She listened intently while I explained about the missing signs and expressed concern when she heard about the Millers' financial problems, Rusty's recent return to the bottle and my long night following his tussle with the county's wealthiest man. Seeing no reason to alarm her, I left out the part about meeting Horace Baker. By the time I'd finished, we had drained our glasses for a second time.

"Any problems setting up your camp?" I tried to sound casual.

"Problems?"

"Any strangers show up? Anyone giving you a hard time?" I didn't like the idea of Horace Baker parked so close to the woman's campsite, but didn't want to raise her fears.

"No worries, boyo." Holly rose and walked over to the fridge, but when I put my hand up, she returned with only one can of stout.

A few minutes later Buck rose from under the table, a loud groan announcing his exit. Kissing Hollyhock on the cheek, I gathered my boots and followed the dog out of the room. At the foot of the stairs, I stopped and said, "Gonna take a quick shower before going to bed. Why don't you sack out in the spare room?"

"Sal-va-torrrre?"

I heard my name, the last syllable emphasized.

Why was Horace Baker calling me?

My mind remained clouded as remnants of sleep slipped past like wisps of early-morning fog sliding over the surface of the pond. Again I heard my name called in that same singsong manner.

I remembered pulling off my moccasins and falling backward onto the bed, closing my eyes, thinking I'd do so for only a few moments, but then Horace Baker had appeared, tramping through my dreams until I could no longer decipher reality from imagination.

"Sal-va-torrrre."

By the time I opened my eyes, the smell of bacon had filled the bedroom. Light streamed through the window overlooking the pond as I sat on the edge of the bed and stared down at my bare feet. I was still dressed in jeans and the flannel shirt that remained damp from my early-morning forays in the rain.

"Wakey, wakey," Hollyhock Leventhal called from the bottom of the stairs.

Padding over to the window, I looked out across the pond, where little wavelets shimmered under a sun that stood high in the sky. Cumulus clouds cast their shadows over the evergreen hills rising beyond the far shoreline. Nearby, the bushes around the cabin glistened with beads of moisture. I stripped off my clothes and wrapped a towel around my waist.

"I have a grand fry cooking," Holly called from the kitchen as I slipped into the shower.

After dressing, I pulled a bottle of ibuprofen from the mirrored cabinet over the bathroom sink and carried it over to the table across from the kitchen.

"You like your rashers crispy?" Holly had the brim of her cap turned backward, breasts jiggling freely, as she bounced around the room in her sneakers.

I tapped out three tablets, washing them down with a sip from the mug of tea she placed in front of me.

The paleontologist had changed into a pair of khaki pants that hung loosely over her round frame and fell to the middle of her calves. The words **UNIVERSITY OF TEL AVIV** were printed in green across the front of a tee that replaced the one she had worn earlier in the morning.

"I meant to ask, is Pru coming to town anytime soon?" She shoveled three slices of bacon onto my plate followed by two eggs.

"I'm always the last to hear about my daughter's comings and goings," I grumbled while breaking off a piece of bacon in my mouth.

"Making a movie. Now tha's brilliant." Holly spooned a pile of fried potatoes onto my dish before sitting down with a plate stacked higher than mine.

"Yeah, tha's brilliant." I did a poor job of mimicking her Irish accent.

"Don't be such an arse." Seeing that I had eaten most of my bacon, Hollyhock added a few more slices to my plate, doing the same for herself.

"You see Buck?" I asked, looking around the room.

"I called for himself earlier, but the old thing trotted outside after he ate and I haven't seen him since."

After cleaning the dishes, we walked out onto the porch.

"Check it out." I handed her the binoculars.

"Will you look at tha', " she mumbled as I grabbed my fleece pullover and tramped down the stairs and out onto the grass that surrounded the cabin, my back and leg stiff.

Hollyhock pulled on a wool sweater she grabbed from the backpack leaning against the green table and followed me outside. As we tramped down to the water's edge a small flock of spring warblers swept into the trees on either side of the path that led down to the pond. I flipped over the longer of my two canoes and held it steady while the paleontologist climbed into the bow. After shoving off, I steered the canoe north and worked my way around the shoreline rather than directly across the pond.

Having moved out of the forest, a large doe panted heavily, her sides heaving, her back arched while she stood in a small clearing. Her winter coat of gray had turned tan, and as the sun rose higher in the sky, we could see the deer's fur bristle as she breathed with difficulty.

Not wanting to spook her, Holly sat quietly while I kept my paddle in the water, maintaining position twenty or so yards from shore. The two of us waited to see if the big doe needed our help, but I had the feeling that this wasn't the first time she was about to bring life into the world.

My sport let out a low "Oh" as the deer lowered her haunches, with first one, and then a second fawn dropping headfirst onto the grass. The sun, which had momentarily receded behind a big puffy cloud, once again appeared, bathing the two quivering bundles of tan-and-white in its warmth, the twins still wrapped in their sticky afterbirth.

I raised my paddle in silent salute, knowing full well that the forest, like a Las Vegas casino, had the odds stacked in its favor, and that those fawns, like you, me and Bailey, the Millers, and Hollyhock Leventhal, were born into a life of suffering, interspersed by a few painfully brief but brilliant moments of incomprehensible joy.

"Fair play to ya," whispered Holly.

The mother's breath had resumed its normal rhythm as she turned to lick her babies. We watched the fawns try to rise, then fall back on their awkward, stick-like legs. Beside them, the doe began to chew on the afterbirth. There were tears in Holly's eyes when she turned back to look in my direction. "Will ya look at those wee ones," she said.

It didn't take long for the two fawns to find their sea legs, staggering around their mother's side, one of them beginning to suckle, the other looking out upon the pond, bewildered, a stranger in a strange land.

For a few minutes my concerns had vanished and for that I was grateful. Buck had been watching from beside meditation boulder, the big dog raising his head as we paddled back to our side of the pond, his wolf-like howl echoing across the water as if in celebration of the fawns' birth.

Chapter Eight

"Mr. D'Amico, can you tell our viewers what you've been doing since writing *Desperadoes of the Mind*?"

The woman with the microphone had walked out from behind a nondescript van parked outside Books-in-the-Woods. Behind her, a guy with long hair pointed a camera in my face. Wearing a pale blue blouse, pinstripe pants and impossibly high heels, the reporter looked to be in her mid-thirties. Tall, slender and quite attractive, she had exceptionally pale skin. She wore her black hair pinned up on her head. I would have been pleased to attract the woman's attention for any reason other than being the latest news story she was assigned to cover.

The two dues-paying members of the fourth estate followed close behind as I walked around the front of the truck's cab, the reporter asking where I'd been living for the last forty years, taking a step back and bumping up against her cameraman when Buck pushed his big head out of the passenger window.

"Your fans would like to know what you've been doing all this time," she quickly recovered.

Ignoring her question, I opened the door of the truck.

"Seems awful heavy." I pointed to the camera.

The long-haired man merely shrugged his shoulders.

A week had passed since Hollyhock Leventhal and I spent the afternoon trolling streamers on Otter Pond. Each day since then I had guided sports on the upper sections of the Magalloway River, spending my nights at the cabin, unable to get back to town until now. A sport staying at Grant's Camps had scheduled a late-afternoon trip on the Kennebago River that would give me the chance to drop in on Bailey, maybe catch up with Ronnie Adams. I had a lot to tell the young warden.

The sun had been shining when I woke, the morning cold but promising fair weather. Singing their songs of renewal, warblers had flashed between the evergreens around the cabin, and notwithstanding the events of the last few weeks, I had been feeling upbeat until the microphone was shoved in my face.

The woman pressed closer, asking a question about my pen name as I opened the truck door. With Buck gathered in my arms, I stooped to the ground, a twinge radiating across my lower back as the big dog's paws touched down on the gravel.

The reporter hesitated when I groaned. After slowly straightening up, I tested my back, gingerly stretching from side to side.

"You okay?" the attractive newswoman asked with what appeared to be genuine concern.

Limping toward the bookstore, I turned to see the woman run a finger across her neck, the guy lowering the camera to the ground. While her colleague lit a cigarette, the reporter pulled out a smartphone, walking first in one direction and then the other, unable to obtain reception.

Inside, Rose trotted out from around the counter and began to nuzzle Buck. Although it was the third week in May, the Jøtul was cranked up high, the big dog walking past the yellow Lab and collapsing on the braided rug in front of the woodstove. Rose circled in frenzied excitement, her tail wagging her hindquarters until she too lay between the stove and the two easy chairs where I spend most of my time when in the store.

Five or six people scanned the tables and shelves with two or three more standing in a line in front of the counter. Business had indeed improved since the film crew had rolled into town.

I expected to find Bailey behind the register, but it was Karen Ross who stood checking out customers. When I drew closer, she whispered, "They're with the movie."

After she finished, Karen walked me toward the back of the store, where the windows overlooked Hawley Pond.

"Can you believe it?" Wayne Ross' ex pointed toward a number of large circus-like tents pitched along the side of the pond. Karen, who supplemented Junior's child support by helping out at the bookstore, told me how her former husband was first to answer the call for extras.

"Wayne says the pay is real good. He says he and some of the other guys from town just sit around all day at the food table, waiting for the few minutes when they're used as background for the real actors."

"Where's Bailey?" I asked.

"Be back sometime after lunch." Karen turned to rush back to the counter, where another line had formed.

Born and raised in the little town, Karen had married, and later divorced, Wayne Ross, who owned Koz's Garage, the town's only gas station, which is where you can find him most spring afternoons unless the "Gone fishin'" sign is hanging in the window. Called Junior by his friends, Karen's former husband kept my battered truck on the road even though its once apple-red exterior now looked more like an orange left out in the sun too long.

I followed her toward the counter. "She say where she was going?"

"Over to Farmington." Karen looked up from the register after bagging a handful of paperback books and handing them to a guy with a straggly beard wearing a hooded jacket with the words **"Chairman Meow"** printed below the face of a red cat.

It wasn't like Bailey to leave the bookstore unless it was really important.

Perplexed as to the reason she would make the ninety-minute round trip to the bigger city, I asked if she had said why.

A woman wearing black stretch pants and an oversized gray sweatshirt walked up to the counter. The sweatshirt had slipped down, revealing a slender shoulder. A man followed a step behind. He had chisled features and a dimple in the middle of his chin that made him look like a young Michael Douglas. He wore a black button-down shirt tucked into white jeans that showed off a hard stomach, wide chest and muscular arms.

"Nope," Karen called past the woman in the black stretch pants, "just that she'd be back before dinner."

The woman attempted to hold back the Michael Douglas look-alike as he stepped in front of me to clear her way toward the counter. Before I could react, the reporter who had approached me outside the store squeezed between us, sticking her microphone in the woman's face.

"This is Danni Donovan and I'm here in the sleepy little hamlet of Easie, located in the backwoods of western Maine, where filming is about to begin on Prudence D'Amico's newest novel. With me is one of the stars of the film..."

Before she could continue, the Michael Douglas look-alike slapped the microphone to the floor, pushing the cameraman hard enough to make him stumble backward.

"Was that really necessary?" When I took a step foward, the guy glared in my direction, but then turned and followed the woman as she slinked past me and out of the store.

I stooped to collect the microphone from the floor. Handing it to the reporter, I said, "Tough morning?"

"Could be worse. Last month I got a cell phone thrown at me."

"You might want to think about a more subtle approach."

The reporter handed the microphone to the cameraman, who was checking his equipment for damage.

"Let's get some lunch," she said to him. "Afterward we'll try by the pond. Maybe we can get something down there."

Danni Donovan turned to me. "How's the food around here?"

"Kim's Pizza Palace is quick and the food's good if you like Italian."

After speaking briefly with the cameraman, she turned back to me. "Larry would prefer a burger and a beer."

"Try the Wooden Nickel. It's just around the corner and down the block."

The two confered for a moment. Afterward, Larry lifted his camera on his shoulder and walked out the door. The woman took out a compact from a small purse that hung from a narrow strap around her shoulder and studied her face. While returning an errant strand of hair behind her ear, she pointed into the mirror and said, "Seems you have fans."

Bending forward to look, I saw two women, one pointing in my direction, the other looking over her shoulder as they stood by the table where my books were displayed.

When I said nothing, Danni Donovan returned the compact to the purse, smiled as if into a camera, and said, "Tell me, Mr. D'Amico, are you going to let a woman eat alone?"

Chapter Nine

Although my morning was shaping up to be anything but normal, the temperature outside the store was typical for late May, in the mid-forties under a sky now shrouded with passing clouds that seemed to race above our heads. The reporter wore a blazer over her silk blouse, and as we passed by my truck, I opened the door and reached inside, grabbing my wool jacket from behind the seat.

"You don't lock your truck?" she asked, her shoulders hunched against the breeze that was coming off Hawley Pond.

"What for? Anyone crazy enough to want the old thing can have it."

Danni Donovan looked puzzled when I handed her the jacket.

"We're gonna walk." I zipped up my fleece pullover, shoving my hands in the pockets of my jeans.

The newswoman held out the wool coat as if it might contain lice, but then draped the jacket over her shoulders as she teetered beside me on heels four inches high. Walking past Lakeview Sports, I noticed Rusty lying under the trailer that held his Rangeley boat. The guide was checking the wooden boat's exterior, something he did after each use to ensure that it remained in pristine condition.

The wind died down when we turned onto Easie Street, where Koos Knyfd smiled from the window of his little shop, the smell of sawdust drifting through the open door. I explained to the reporter that using only a chainsaw, the old Swede had carved the twelve-foot wooden bear that stood outside the town.

"We on for tomorrow?" Sam Treadwell called from outside his office. The veterinarian sat on a bench, his face turned up to the sun that had peeked through a break in the clouds, his long legs crossed at the ankles, a coffee mug held between his hands.

"Do you mind if we make a quick detour?" I asked while guiding Donovan across the gravel-and-dirt main street of town.

She extended her hand toward the veterinarian as I introduced one to the other. Arthur Wentworth, Sr., a cigarette clutched between his rotting teeth, smirked as he sauntered past. I watched the elder Wentworth walk up the stairs of Ollie's store, where Joe Hawley's grounds crew sat around tables eating their lunches.

"Six-thirty," I replied to Sam, who had turned toward the deck of the general store at the sound of a whistle, a few of the men grinning in our direction.

"Have you seen Ronnie?" I asked.

"You just missed him. He stopped by Ollie's to pick up lunch before driving back out of town."

As we talked, Wayne Ross trotted up the street. Ignoring Donovan, he asked, "We still on?"

I repeated what I'd said to Sam.

"You bringing J.J.?" the vet asked.

"You kidding? He can't wait."

On the way back across the street I recounted the first time Wayne Ross pulled his Camaro into Koz's Garage. Donovan listened as I told her how the owner of the station gave the kid from New Jersey a job pumping gas while allowing the teenager to live in the apartment above the gas station.

"Koz taught Wayne everything he knew about engines, treating him like the son he never had, and it wasn't long before people in town began calling the kid Koz Junior. The name stuck, although over the years it's been shortened to Junior."

"And J.J.?" she asked.

"When Wayne had a son, someone called the kid Junior Junior, which morphed into J.J. It just seemed natural."

"Natural?" she repeated the word, turning it into a question while staring up at the hot-pink neon sign that proclaimed Andrew Kim's pizza to be the best north of Brooklyn.

Inside, we found an open booth and slid onto the red plastic seats on either side of a Formica table. The newswoman slipped off my coat while scanning a menu she found wedged between a jar of grated cheese and another of oregano. A moment later, a slender teenager with a dark complexion and attractive smile walked over to take our order. The youngest of Finley and Beldora MacDougall's three daughters held a pen in one hand and a small notepad in the other. Her midnight-black hair was parted down the middle and bound in two long braids. Sanrevelle MacDougall had grown into a younger version of her mother, a no-nonsense Portuguese beauty.

"The usual, Mr. D'Amico?" she asked.

"Sounds good, Sandy."

As a child, Sanrevelle enjoyed spending time on the water, her father and I taking the young girl with us whenever we went fishing. Since turning fourteen, she worked after school at Ollie's General Store and on weekends at Kim's, the boys in town competing for whatever free time remained.

"And for you, ma'am?" The youngster looked down at Danni Donovan, pen poised above her pad.

The reporter looked at me from over the menu, and I was fairly certain that if a man wasn't careful, he might drown in those blue eyes.

"So what's the usual?" she asked.

"Two slices of cheese pizza and a root beer," interrupted Sanrevelle.

"Make mine with pepperoni and I'll have a Diet Coke." Donovan returned the menu to the side of the table and once again fixed those doe-like eyes on mine.

Lowering her chin onto raised hands, she smiled and said, "You're a strange man, Salvatore D'Amico."

"How's that?"

"Well, it seems that back in the day you achieved everything I'm fighting to obtain, and then you..." She hesitated, trying to find the right word to describe how I chucked it all in for a life as a fishing guide.

"Really, and what exactly is it that ace reporter Danni Donovan is trying so hard to achieve?" I stared back at her.

While the reporter's eyes continued to hold mine, she thought about my question, shifting them away only when Sandy returned, the young girl placing straws alongside two large plastic glasses that she lowered to our table.

After prying off the paper, Donovan sank one of the straws between the ice cubes that bobbed along the top of the glass.

"Success and all the things that go along with it," she said, once Sanrevelle was out of earshot.

"And ambushing people with a camera is how you intend to get those things?"

The newswoman twirled the straw around the inside of her glass.

After a moment, she said, "Unless you're Barbara Walters or Katie Couric, it's impossible to get a celebrity to sit for an interview."

I took a long drink, savoring the bittersweet taste of the root beer. Setting the glass down, I said, "There must be a better way."

The reporter laughed, thought for a moment, and then added, "You have no idea."

It was my turn to chuckle. We might have different values and probably had little in common, but I found myself attracted to this woman with the charming smile and captivating eyes.

"And the whole stick-a-microphone-in-someone's-face thing has worked for you?" I persisted, as Sanrevelle returned with four slices of steaming pizza.

The newswoman shrugged her shoulders while shaking the jar of grated cheese over her slice. She did the same with the jar of oregano, blowing on the pizza before taking an enormous bite.

"I suppose there's one thing we can agree on." I smiled, raising my slice from its paper plate.

"And that would be?" the reporter mumbled, her mouth full.

"We both like pizza."

"That we do." Danni Donovan replied between another sip from her straw and a second large bite from the slice she had raised to her lips.

After that, we decided to call a truce, electing to find neutral subjects to discuss. When Sandy brought the bill, I insisted on paying, and was digging in the front pocket of my jeans when the newswoman pointed toward the door.

"Do you know who that is?" she asked in a hushed tone.

I turned to look over my shoulder as a tiny man walked up to the counter. Three men and two women hovered around him like five planets rotating around a diminutive sun.

A thin elastic strap held a black patch over the little man's left eye. The strap pressed down around thick blond hair that flowed from under a wide-brimmed black fedora that he wore cocked to one side. His goatee was the same color as the hair that swept over his ears and down his shoulders in a series of golden waves, the tips of his moustache curling upward into waxed points. Except for his single eye and the fact that he stood no taller than four feet, he reminded me of a photograph I'd once seen of George Armstrong Custer.

The boy at the register called to the owner of the pizzeria, who appeared from the back of the store, wiping flour from his hands as he approached the miniature solar system. The apron spread around the Korean's waist and over his sleeveless T-shirt was stained with tomato sauce. After a brief discussion, Kim pointed a finger in our direction.

"That's Bruno Magalini," Donovan whispered as the little star shifted his light toward our table, the five heavenly bodies continuing to wobble in orbit around him.

"Who?" I watched as the golden orb drew closer.

"They call him the Great Magalini. He's directing your daughter's film." She rose when the planetary system began to adjust itself alongside our table.

"Salvatore D'Amico?" The director extended his stubby fingers in my direction, pronouncing the last two letters of my first name as "ray."

Bemused, I remained seated. "Can I help you?" I said.

"You are Salvatore D'Amico, the great author and the father of Prudence D'Amico."

"Not sure about the great author part, but I'm Prudence's dad."

When I heard the newswoman clear her throat, I added, "And this is Danni Donovan, a reporter with..." I stopped and turned toward her.

"It's an honor, an honor to meet you, Mr. Magalini."

I was surprised to hear a tremor in Donovan's voice when she told the director the name of her local station. The little man nodded and then once again focused his bright light in my direction.

"Mr. D'Amico, I'm sure you realize that my film is as much about your life as it is about your daughter's novel."

Before I could reply, the director asked to spend the next afternoon on the water with me. When I explained that I was booked for the day, the maestro wouldn't take no for an answer, stating that he would pay five times my going rate if I could find a way to break free.

I looked across at the reporter and thought for a moment before dictating my conditions, which the Great Magalini accepted without hesitation.

Chapter Ten

After agreeing to guide the director, I walked Danni Donovan back to the bookstore, where Larry, a cigarette between his fingers, leaned against their van. As we approached, he flipped the cigarette away and leaned down to retrieve the large camera from the ground beside him.

After reclaiming my coat, I checked on Buck, who was still stretched out in front of the Jøtul stove, and then walked down to Lakeview Sports.

Inside, I pointed to the three or four people walking around the aisles and asked Jeanne Miller if business had picked up.

"Not nearly enough to bring our loan current by the end of the month."

"I may be able to help with that. Rusty in?" I asked.

She nodded.

I found her husband in his office at the back of the store, where he was cleaning fly lines. Rusty listened while I told him about Magalini's generous offer. Happy for the few extra bucks, the guide agreed to take on my sports for the following afternoon while I spent time with the director. I asked him if he had seen Ronnie Adams, but he hadn't.

I knew our game warden would be interested in the dead fish strewn along the bank of the Little Magalloway as well as the missing sign on Green Top. More importantly, he'd want to know that Horace Baker was out of jail. So, before collecting my sport, I decided to stop at Koz's Garage. Not only was

Wayne Ross' gas station the place where most rumors in town came to gestate, it was also where many of them were born. If anyone knew the whereabouts of the local warden it would be Junior.

While topping off my tank, the young mechanic described how he and Merle Lansing had hired on as extras, more for the food than the money. I listened to his description of the tent city that had sprung up along the edge of Hawley Pond. According to Wayne, most of the tents housed cameras and lights as well as all types of expensive electrical and computer equipment, the crew and technicians far outnumbering the actors. Other tents contained the food services, which, he said, were quite lavish. He explained that when not in front of the cameras or back in their rooms at the Hawley Inn, the principal players remained sequestered in fancy trailers parked along the shore of the pond.

When I asked about Ronnie, Wayne told me the warden had been in to the station to gas up his vehicle no more than ten minutes before, but had headed right back out. Wayne said Ronnie had complained that to the exclusion of their other duties, the local wardens were ordered to patrol the logging roads around Mooselookmeguntic in an effort to stop the removal of signs along the big lake.

"After the paper companies put pressure on Augusta, the governor ordered the wardens to catch The Bear."

"The Bear?"

"You've heard about the claw marks? No one knows for sure, but people have taken to calling whoever or whatever is responsible The Bear."

I thought about trying to track Ronnie down, but the network of logging roads that spread deep into the forest around the Rangeley Lakes was vast and the chances of locating him slim.

Bailey had not returned when I stopped back at Books-in-the-Woods, but Karen agreed to look after Buck until I returned from my trip up the Kennebago. The more I thought about it, Bailey hadn't looked well over the last week or so. The closest doctor worked out of a clinic located in Rangeley, but neither Rangeley nor Easie had its own pharmacy, a real hardship for seniors and others who didn't drive, and I wondered if that's why she left the store to make the long trip south to Farmington.

Worry bore down upon me like the dark clouds of an approaching storm. With friends on the brink of foreclosure, a dangerous poacher mucking around and Bailey acting out of sorts, it was awfully hard to stay in the moment. I wondered how the Buddha did it. After turning off Route 16, I humped over the logging road that flanked the Kennebago River.

I found my sport standing outside the main lodge of Grant's Camps. Extending his hand, he greeted me with a nervous smile. In his mid-fifties, he wore expensive chest waders with every conceivable tool hanging from a vest that appeared new. Shorter than me, he had pale skin but looked in good shape. He reminded me of a vole, the way his eyes were too small for his head. When he lifted his cap, I could see that his sandy blond hair was cut short.

I'm often amazed at the assortment of flies and other tackle my sports carry. I suppose it's necessary on technical rivers like the Housatonic or the West Branch of the Delaware, where suspicious brown trout will only rise to the tiniest of patterns tied to exacting imitation and knotted to tippets as thin as a spider's thread. Although our fish require fortitude to seek them out in the wild places where they tend to reside and a degree of stealth when we approach them, the brook trout of western Maine are not overly particular when it comes to dining, and most flies cast with a drag-free drift will bring success. The key is not so much the amount of gear as knowing how to use what little you have.

Sitting beside me in the Toyota, Günter Henderson explained that he had fished for many years, but until his divorce, only on local streams. A civil engineer, he worked for the city of Hartford, Connecticut. Booking time at Grant's, he hoped I'd show him the pools along the river, allowing him to fish on his own during the remainder of his stay.

"You picked the right week," I told him. "The fish are in the river and they're active."

He tightened his lips as we bounced down the camp road.

Starting at the Lower Abutment Pool, we swung our streamers across the tannin-stained current, continuing upriver through many of the runs known to the camp owners on Big Kennebago Lake. Working through Morrison's Pool, Wire Pool and Cedar Pool, Günter cast his five-weight, nine-foot rod with precision and, although more comfortable with small flies tied to fine tippets, he quickly adjusted to the larger bucktail I had knotted to his line. The purple-and-black streamer caught the attention of the trout, and during four hours on the river my sport released a number of fish that kept him entertained, including two brook trout, one fourteen inches long, the other sixteen, and a salmon measuring somewhere in between.

Sometime after four, I noticed a few splashes at the head of Pine Stump Pool and clipped off my sport's streamer in favor of a small gray caddis with a CDC wing. When a good-looking fish swirled under his fly, Günter set the hook, a silver-and-white torpedo bursting through the surface, tail dancing alongside the far bank. A few minutes later I slipped my long-handled net under a fat salmon that brought a smile to my sport's face, the first since we shook hands and one that remained with him during the drive back to the lodge.

By the time we settled up, the sun had begun its descent, the hills to the east of Kennebago Lake bathed in gentle light. As we shook hands, a young girl wearing jeans and a Metallica T-shirt stood outside Grant's main lodge ringing the dinner bell. She ran quickly back inside the kitchen, goose bumps on her arms.

The sun had set by the time I pulled into the little clearing around my cabin. A pair of loons called to each other from either end of the pond while I gathered my gear and hitched the trailer carrying my sixteen-foot Grumman to my truck. I'd need the bigger boat to guide the director on the lake, and although Aziscohos was closer to my camp, I had seen Bailey less than usual and still hoped to spend the night with her.

I managed to pull in front of Books-in-the-Woods a little before nine that evening. It took a while to maneuver the rig beside the curb, but after doing so I walked under the light that illuminated the sign beside the bookstore's door and up the stairs to Bailey's apartment. I was looking forward to spending some time together, but after finding her curled up in bed, I decided against it. After letting the dogs out for a final sniff of fresh air, I prepared a meal for my outing with Magalini and ate a cold dinner sometime after eleven. Bailey didn't stir when I slipped into bed beside her.

Rising early, Bailey had dressed and walked downstairs, opening the store while I was still in the shower. From the deck of her apartment, I watched sunlight dapple the surface of Hawley Pond. Beside the pond, I could make out the cast and crew's vehicles tucked in among the complex of tents and trailers Junior had described the previous afternoon. I counted a few newer-model SUVs and American trucks as well as a number of other expensive cars. Most were black, *the newest rage in Hollywood*, I thought.

I recognized Junior's red pickup, a late-model Ford Ranger, and Merle Lansing's powder blue Subaru with the dent in the passenger-side door. Both were parked among other older vehicles in a lot along the edge of the encampment.

The weather had moderated overnight, the breeze coming off the pond not as cold as the day before. The temperature had edged up into the mid-fifties. It would be a fine day for Magalini to be on the water. Sliding the glass door open, I stepped back inside Bailey's apartment and over Buck's prone body, the old dog raising his head, and then quickly lowering it again with a grunt.

Although particular about my tea, I have fairly simple taste, preferring Tetley's British blend, which comes in oval bags, although Lipton's standard brew will also do in a pinch. Irish breakfast tea is a nice change of pace, as is Earl Grey, but none of those fruity blends and never green tea. The water must be boiled in a pot on a stove and not in a microwave, although Bailey prefers an electric kettle favored by the British, which I now used for my second mug of the morning.

The previous evening I had packed a red-and-white cooler with Magalini's lakeside lunch. I checked it again while finishing my tea. Grabbing my fleece pullover, I slipped past Buck, leaving the old dog to bake in the morning sun, and lumbered down the steps of the apartment. Through the window of the bookstore, I found Bailey standing behind the counter chatting with her tenant, Martha Dudley, the younger woman who rented the apartment beside hers. The two women appeared to abort their conversation, Martha looking over her shoulder with a nervous smile when I walked into the store.

"Buck's asleep." I lowered the cooler to the floor and scratched Rose's chin. "He may need to go out in an hour or so."

When Bailey didn't answer, I asked her if everything was okay. I had wanted to tell her about my lunch with the pretty reporter and that I'd be out late fishing with the guys, but hadn't had the opportunity.

Rose wagged her tail wildly as I moved my hand toward her belly.

"Everything's fine," Bailey replied, grabbing the phone on its first ring. Lowering the receiver, she said, "I've got to take this."

Questions were beginning to tumble one against the other like a row of dominoes. I wanted to ask what she had been doing down in Farmington and why she was keeping her distance from me and what the hell was bothering her. Instead, I turned toward the store's open door and said, "Be back after dark."

Adept at reading water, however dark and mysterious, and finding it easy to solve the puzzle of often confusing and overlapping hatches that bring trout out to play, I'm lost when it comes to deciphering a woman's intentions. Bailey seemed out of sorts, even distant, which was not like her. She didn't even ask why I'd be late.

Martha waved as I walked out of the store, Bailey quickly turning her attention back to the phone. Out on the street, I looked down at my boot, where a white stone caught my eye. Dropping to one knee, I ran my thumb over a green vein that ran through the small rock, slipping it into the pocket of my jeans. After checking the trailer hitch and the straps around the Grumman, I slid the cooler onto the floor below the passenger seat and pulled away from the store.

I turned right at Lakeview Sports and drove over the bridge that traverses the Hawley River. The sun continued to shine down between clouds that were large and puffy, and I rolled down the truck's window, thinking about the day when I had first met Bailey. It was on a similar afternoon, a few months after she first arrived in Easie driving a beat-up car, its backseat piled high with possessions, a greenish-blue band of color orbiting around her bruised eye like Saturn's rings.

Turning west on Route 16, I passed Koos Knyfd's twelve-foot wooden bear. A familiar clatter filled the truck's cab as the lightweight trailer carrying the square-stern aluminum canoe bounced along the blacktop.

Bailey had purchased a new Wrangler about the time her black eye had healed. On the day we first met she had steered the Jeep out of the path of a young moose, driving into a drainage ditch not far from Otter Brook. On that afternoon more than nine years ago, the weather had turned brisk, and in preparation for the long hike out to the blacktop, Bailey had removed her cutoffs, leaning back into the vehicle, searching for her jeans at about the time I walked up the road with Buck.

A few miles outside of town while still thinking about that afternoon, I stopped at the bridge that straddles the Kennebago River. Staring downstream, I couldn't remember whether it was Bailey's emerald eyes staring up at me in surprise or the red panties that were barely covered by the bottom of her flannel shirt, but like Ralph Rich coming upon Louise Dickinson along the Rapid River, I was hers from that first encounter.

Lingering on the bridge, I followed the course of the tannin-stained current until it swung around a bend where it would soon join the Cupsuptic River, the two streams forming the headwaters above Cupsuptic Lake, the northern finger of Mooselookmeguntic Lake.

Before meeting Bailey, I had been content to live in my cabin by the pond with a good dog by my side, a few friends to tell tales of my time on the water, and the occasional woman to share my bed whenever the need arose. Although she might be the best thing that ever wandered across my path, that didn't mean I understood her. Instead, I decided early on to let her be, ride the wave, as Richard Morrell liked to say. Up until now, I had enjoyed the ride, enjoyed it very much. It was only lately that I seemed to have lost my footing.

Chapter Eleven

Passing the Morton Cutoff Road, I continued west on Route 16, driving another twenty minutes on the blacktop before turning onto the Lincoln Pond logging road. Not long afterward, I pulled my truck into the dirt lot at the entrance of the Black Brook Cove Campgrounds. Stopping in front of the campgrounds' general store, I backed the trailer toward the boat ramp beside the cove that curls around the southeastern arm of Aziscohos Lake like a cat sleeping alongside a woodstove. Boats bobbed on either side of a short wooden dock. Along the edge of the cove the leaves of the hardwood trees were now big enough to rustle in the modest breeze that came off the water.

A few feet away, an African-American man wearing dark slacks and a white, short-sleeve, button-down shirt leaned against the front fender of a black Tahoe. Although he was not very tall, perhaps five-ten, his arms and shoulders reminded me of the Incredible Hulk. He wore sunglasses and a thin black tie. His salt-and-pepper hair was cut short. He looked familiar, but I couldn't place him.

As I eased the trailer down the earthen ramp, the man plodded toward the rear of the SUV and opened the door. A moment later the Great Magalini appeared, his blond hair flowing down from under his black fedora, the wide-brimmed hat once again tipped to the side. Smoke rose in a thin column from a long, thin, brown-papered cigarette that he held between his pudgy fingers.

The famous director said something to the man, who nodded and then walked around the back of the vehicle. As Magalini turned in my direction, I bent forward to pick up a large dun-colored feather that was floating along the edge of the waterline.

"What do you have there, Mr. D'Amico?" he asked.

"It's from a great blue heron." I tucked the feather's shaft into my breast pocket.

Bruno Magalini wore a red shirt with two columns of brass buttons running down his chest. He had his sleeves rolled to the elbows, his khaki pants tucked into brown leather boots that were laced up to his knees. Standing with his face raised toward the sun, his arms folded against his chest, the maestro looked more like *Il Duce* than the flamboyant post-Civil War general who made his last stand on a hilltop not far from a trout stream called the Little Bighorn River.

The man with the muscular arms and wide chest trod toward the dock as I unlashed the Grumman from the trailer. He carried a duffel bag in one large hand and a rod tube in another. While the director conferred with his chauffeur, I slid the boat into the water, unlocking the four-horsepower engine and lowering it against the boat's transom. I noticed a slight hitch in the man's stride when he trudged back to the Tahoe. I was still trying to place him when the director called out, "And LeBron, don't forget to tell Sophia to be ready for the shoot tonight. Oh, and call Harry, be certain that he has Jennifer in makeup and sober. We don't want that full moon to go to waste."

If life were a cartoon, a lightbulb would have appeared over my head. I suddenly recalled a snowy afternoon in mid-December. Was it three, or four years back? The fullback for the San Francisco 49ers had scored three touchdowns in a playoff game against the Chicago Bears before breaking his leg in the closing minutes. During the weeks that followed, I found myself cringing each time the news replayed LeBron Hayes' career-ending injury.

After securing the Grumman between two pilings, I trotted back up to the lot and parked the Toyota behind the general store where the trailer would be out of the way. Removing the red-and-white cooler from the cab, I reached into the truck's bed, grabbed the sections of two trolling rods and carried them back toward the dock, my rucksack slung over my shoulder. Leaning down, I arranged our gear in the bow of the boat. I could hear the director's heels clomping against the wooden planks of the dock and looked up to see the little man pulling out a cell phone from his shirt pocket. He raised it over his head and then, extending his arms, pointed it in different directions until I explained that the nearest tower was somewhere on the other side of the mountains that rose above the western horizon.

I held the aluminum craft against the dock until my sport took his seat. After a few pulls of the cord, the outboard sputtered into action. LeBron slipped one rope free of a cleat beside the bow while I loosened a second rope from a piling by the stern. A moment later the Grumman cut gracefully through the surface as we slowly progressed through the cove and out into the southern tip of the lake.

The director was interested in my personal story, asking questions about my early life, how I came to the region and why I chose to abandon a career as a writer. Steering him away from the subject, I pointed out that as the most western of the bodies of water that comprise the Rangeley Lakes Region, parts of the lake's shoreline border New Hampshire. Undeterred, he asked whether I was still in touch with Gary Snyder or any of my other friends from the sixties and seventies. Ignoring his question, I explained that the concrete dam creating the long and narrow impoundment was the largest structure of its kind when built in 1911.

Once he realized that I wasn't going to divulge anything about my personal life, Magalini leaned forward and removed a small device that I mistook for a smartphone, until he pointed it in my direction.

"Remarkable," I concluded my history of the dam as he pointed the digital voice recorder in my direction, "considering that the nearest railway was located more than forty miles away, and supplies and equipment had to be hauled in by horses from the tiny hamlet of Wilsons Mills."

As we worked our way along the shoreline, the director recorded my commentary about the lake, its fishery and the flora and fauna along its banks. Although the air was crisp, the sun remained strong, the temperature continuing to rise. I slipped on a pair of polarized sunglasses that has survived loss over many years. The maestro did the same, pulling from his breast pocket one of those futuristic wrap-around models favored by younger guides and professional athletes.

My sport began to take in the scenery, asking questions about the region while recording my answers as well as his comments on the little gadget. When he returned the tiny device to his duffel and pulled out an expensive-looking digital camera, I reduced speed to allow him to take photographs of the surrounding hills and the more distant northern mountains that rose from Canadian soil.

As we approached a rocky spit of land, I shifted the outboard into neutral and began rigging one of the trolling rods. Magalini continued to snap pictures of the conifer-studded island while I knotted a Grey Ghost to a three-foot section of five-pound-test monofilament attached to one end of a brass swivel. Putting aside his camera, the director once again grabbed his recorder, pushing in the button on the tiny machine while asking about the streamer, one of many that I had tied upon a set of tandem hooks during the previous winter.

I told him the tale known to most anglers throughout New England, the one concerning Wallace Stevens, the preeminent guide during the early part of the twentieth century, and his wife, Carrie. I explained that their summer cottage was called Camp Midway, and how it was located across from Upper Dam, the large wooden structure that separated Mooselookmeguntic and

Richardson Lakes, the place where Carrie Stevens created various streamer patterns that have been copied long after her death. He kept his recorder running as I described the record-breaking brook trout Carrie reportedly caught using a pattern similar to the one knotted to his line and how an article in *Field & Stream* magazine resulted in her fame forever eclipsing that of her husband.

While recounting the story of Wallace and Carrie, I attached the end of the swivel to thirty more feet of monofilament, which was connected to an old, cracked floating fly line that was no longer serviceable on a trout stream, but worked perfectly well as a trolling line. Magalini stated that he was an avid fly fisher, well acquainted with the rivers out West, where he cast his flies to big browns and rainbows, but that he had never trolled for fish in a lake and was looking forward to catching his first landlocked salmon.

Rigging the second rod, I described how our streamers would extend eighty or more feet beyond the stern of the Grumman while descending no more than a few feet below the surface. When the director asked why we didn't lower them deeper, I explained that although the smelt had settled back into the lake after concluding their spawning run, this early in the spring, Maine's principal baitfish would remain within a few feet of the surface, where the water was only beginning to warm, which is where the salmon would seek them out.

I told him how the smelt would migrate to deeper depths once the water grew warmer, the heat gradually driving both prey and predator to the bottom of the lake until the fall, when they could once again be found near the surface.

Handing the director one of the trolling rods, I slid the other into a metal holder secured to the side of the Grumman. After a few minutes passed without a strike, Magalini lowered his rod, clasping it between his knees while snapping a photograph of two wood ducks huddled behind some reeds. As we continued around the far side of the island, I pointed to a pair of loons, one bird diving under the surface while the other preened, its long black beak nervously pecking through its shank feathers.

When the salmon hit, the long trolling rod bent forward, slipping from between the maestro's knees. When he reached out to retrieve it, the recording device slipped out of his shirt pocket, the camera falling from his hands. Lunging forward, I grabbed the butt before the rod could fall overboard, handing it back to the director, who ignored his expensive equipment clanging against the bottom of the aluminum boat.

"Wait for it," I whispered, pointing over my shoulder, where sixty feet or so behind the Grumman's stern a black-and-silver flash exploded through the surface like a ballistic missile. When the salmon leaped a second time, the fish, perhaps three feet in the air, flung the streamer in one direction while splashing down on its side in the other.

The director stared back at me, his one good eye open wide, the lifeless rod held in his trembling hands.

"That, Mr. Magalini, was one of our smaller salmon."

Chapter Twelve

We had cruised the lake for the better part of four hours, Magalini taking a number of short salmon as well as one that measured over twenty inches, the director complaining like a petulant child when I released the fish without removing it from the water.

For the next hour the maestro pouted, his sour mood only improving after he drank his second glass of Merlot. The wine had accompanied a lunch of grouse sautéed in a white wine sauce. I had cooked the bird while at Bailey's apartment, wrapping it with a few white potatoes in an insulated bag packed into the cooler, heating them over coals on the shoreline. The two birds were obtained in a trade with Junior Ross for two dozen of my Gold-Ribbed Hare's Ear wet flies, my own variation on a traditional pattern that I tie with an underbody of red silk.

LeBron Hayes was waiting beside the boat ramp when we returned. He carried my sport's duffel back to the Tahoe and opened the back door for the director. The shorter man's gait reminded me of a duck as he waddled toward the SUV. After the chauffeur closed the door, the tinted window slipped down, the former pro athlete calling me over to the vehicle.

Surprised when he told me that Magalini wanted to book the following day on the water, I nevertheless agreed, figuring Rusty could use the money he'd earn guiding the sports previously scheduled to fish with me. Pulling off my cap, I ran my fingers through my hair, watching as the Tahoe pulled up the short drive and turned onto the logging road, a wave of grit and dust unfurling in the vehicle's wake. The breeze had died away, the sun shifting toward the west, bathing the hills that marked the border between New Hampshire and the state of Maine with a golden hue. A few yards away a chipmunk scampered across the trunk of a tree that had fallen along the edge of the forest. Above, a chickadee called, another answering from a nearby spruce.

I was scheduled to meet Sam and Junior Ross later in the evening. With time to kill, I wandered up the path toward the general store and opened the screen door. Inside, a tall man gripped a toothpick between his teeth. He wore a green shirt and beat-up cap of the same color, and was bent over a counter drawing directions on the back of a napkin while another man dressed in a sweatshirt and cargo shorts listened intently.

As the screen door slammed behind me, Jeff Lafleur looked up. He removed the toothpick from the corner of his mouth and nodded in my direction. Looking back down at his makeshift map, he returned the toothpick, using his tongue to slide the tapered piece of wood from one side of his mouth to the other, while resuming his conversation. The previous spring, Jeff and I had explored the little brook that he had drawn on the napkin. The guy in the cargo shorts was in for some good fishing.

Before I could advance closer, two dervishes came whirling through the open door of the backroom followed by a German shorthaired pointer that bounded behind them. The Lafleur children, ages three and five, bounced off my shins while the dog did her best to squeeze between them.

"Jennie, Jake!" A petite woman with dark eyes, her legs spread apart, stood beside the door. Barbara Lafleur had removed a pair of work gloves and held them in one hand while grasping a trowel in the other. The bill of her green baseball cap stood up high, a few locks of her short auburn hair slipping down over her brow.

Upon hearing her voice, the dog backed off, sitting on her haunches, a nub of a tail wagging with anticipation while the two younger Lafleurs, ignoring their mother's command, attempted to climb up each of my legs.

"Sorry, Sal." Barbara Lafleur marched forward in a vain effort to restrain her children. She wore jeans with muddy knees, a denim work shirt and work boots scuffed from long use. Despite her attire, she could never be mistaken for a man, her shapely body and pretty face ample evidence of her femininity.

I picked up Jake, who grabbed the heron feather from my shirt. With my free hand, I felt around in the pocket of my jeans, pulling out the white stone with the jagged green vein running through its center, and handed it to his sister.

"You know the island about a mile up the lake?" I asked them.

"Where Pa likes to troll?" the boy asked.

"That's the one. Well, I was out there this afternoon and I stopped to chat with this blue heron I know."

"Birds don't talk." Jennie frowned while staring down at the tiny rock I had found earlier that morning.

"This one does," I replied, avoiding her mother's stare.

By now the kids had settled down, Jake staring up at me, his eyes the same color as his mother's and as wide as the circles of a trout's rise, Jennie holding the stone up to the light, one eye closed, the other squinting at the tiny rock.

"Haven't you met Winslow?" I looked down at the older sibling, who appeared puzzled.

"Winslow?" She glanced back at her mother, who shrugged her shoulders, rolling her eyes after Jennie turned back in my direction.

"Winslow's been around since before people came to the forests and lakes. Back when faeries lived in the trees and under the boulders." I lowered Jake to the floor.

"Faeries?" The boy looked puzzled; his sister's frown broadened as she once more looked down at the stone in her open palm.

"Faeries. You know, like elves. Back then, Winslow had been the king wizard. Like the other wizards, he could talk with the trees and all the animals, even the fish."

"I've never seen any faeries. Where'd they all go anyways?" Jake asked.

"Well, they didn't mind the Native Americans so much, but when our ancestors came to these forests and started killing off the animals and logging the trees, they decided to cross over the border into Canada."

"Canada?"

"Sure. But then the faeries learned that they would have to speak French."

The guy in the cargo shorts had turned around and was now listening, hiding his smile when Jennie looked over at her father.

"So the Queen Faerie decided on another plan. You know how butterflies fly thousands of miles each year to spend their winter in South America?"

"You remember, Jakie. I showed you those pictures of the different butterflies in that big book we took out of the library." Jeff Lafleur leaned across the counter, his customer nodding in agreement.

Jake and Jennie turned from their father back to me.

"You see, the faeries had always gotten along well with the butterflies and when the great queen proclaimed it was time to leave, they just climbed atop their butterfly friends and flew south."

"What happened to Winslow and the other wizards?" Jake asked.

"The faeries offered to take the wizards with them, but the wizards were too fat to fly on the backs of butterflies and although very wise, they too had trouble speaking French, preferring the languages of the animals."

"I didn't know animals spoke different languages." Barbara had gathered the two children by her side, dark eyes sparkling as she waited for my reply.

"Um, okay." I hesitated for a moment. "Same language, but the moose, deer and black bear speak one dialect while otters, weasels and minks speak another, the smaller animals like mice, voles and moles speaking still another."

"What about the fish?" Jake cried out.

"The fish have a completely different language as do the birds, and the trees and plants, but the wizards could speak them all, although they preferred bird to the others."

"That right?" muttered the guy by the counter.

"But when the faeries left, they took their magic faerie dust with them. After that, the plants and animals could only speak each with their own kind. Even the wizards found it hard to converse in the different dialects and languages that had once rolled so easily off their tongues. Rather than learn French, they decided to disguise themselves as herons and remain in the forest, where they had lived since before the beginning of time."

"What do you and Winslow talk about?" Jake showed no trace of his sister's skepticism.

"You know what good fishermen herons are?"

"Sure," he warbled.

"Well, from time to time I ask Winslow's advice, especially on an off-day."

"Is that what you were talking about today?" Jennie was reserving judgment.

"Today I told the heron where he could find a school of chub and as a thank-you he plucked out that feather"—I pointed toward the dun-colored feather that the little boy waved above his head—"and gave me that." I pointed toward the stone in the palm of his sister's hand. "He said they were magic."

"You never told me you speak bird," Barbara muttered as she bent down to collect her son.

"Yeah. I thought you only spoke fish," added Jeff from behind the counter.

After rolling up the napkin with the directions written on it, the sport thanked Jeff for the information, tipped his cap in my direction and walked out the front door of the store.

"Son of a bitch," the store's owner mumbled loud enough for all of us to hear.

"Jeff!" Barbara stared at her husband over the heads of their children.

"Well hell, ya'd think he might have bought a few flies or at least a piece of jerky."

An angler seeking details about an unfamiliar river or pond should know better than to expect a local shop owner to give away his secret fishing hole, but many, like Jeff Lafleur, will share what is common knowledge to those living nearby, and it's only good manners to purchase a few items from the store in return for such information indispensible to someone who may have only a day or two to learn new water.

"Put in your lettuce yet?" Barbara decided to change the subject while raising one hand to ward off the feather Jake waved in her face.

"Is this really a magic stone?" The little girl wrinkled up her nose.

"Not yet. Think I'll wait another week," I replied to the mother, and to the daughter said, "You never know with Winslow, but it's possible."

"Guess I best get back to it." Barbara Lafleur took her daughter by the hand, and with her son in the other arm, called the dog to her side.

While Jeff's wife herded her brood out the back door, I walked over to the wall beside the counter and opened one of three plastic containers arranged on a shelf. Broken into small compartments, each held different flies—one for dries, another for nymphs and wets and the third for streamers. Most were traditional patterns, workhorses that stood the test of time like Wooly Buggers and Muddler Minnows, but the store's owner also stocked local patterns like Fern Bosse's Sneeka, a streamer I have used with great success, and my own pattern, the Drunken Lady.

"You look a little low," I muttered, lowering the lid on the box.

"Think I'll wait a bit before reordering." Jeff walked out from behind the counter, adjusting boxes of doughnuts, bags of potato chips and other staples that lined the single aisle of the small store. I noticed that there were no more than one or two of any particular item and surmised that it had been a while since he had restocked much of anything.

"Thanks for the use of the boat launch." I pulled a ten-dollar bill out of my wallet and handed it to the younger man.

"Any luck?" he added.

"Fair to middlin'." I gave my usual response, adding, "Lost a salmon off Birch Island. Took a few shorts farther up the lake, released a nice one at the Ledges."

"I heard Rusty's havin' a tough time." Jeff opened the glass-lined freezer along the back wall of the store, stacking it with six-packs of beer.

As if carried by red squirrels, word spread quickly through the balsam-and-spruce forest.

"Speaking of which, can I use your phone?"

Jeff grabbed his landline and set it on the counter. I dialed the number for Lakeview Sports. When Jeanne answered, she confirmed that her husband would meet the three sports I was scheduled to guide on the following day.

"Everyone in town is hoping business will pick up now that the film crew has arrived," I said, sliding the phone back toward Jeff.

"Half my campsites are empty," he replied.

"Tom Rider says bookings are down from last year." I looked into a bin that contained a few fresh rolls.

Jeff climbed onto a stool behind the counter. "Someone poached a deer a few nights back. Found dried blood on the logging road and followed the trail into the woods, where I found a pile of offal a few feet away from some kernels of corn."

"You know Horace's back?" I asked, grabbing a long roll from the bin.

Jeff looked up from a back issue of *The Maine Sportsman* he had opened.

"Saw evidence of fish taken with worms up on the Little Mag same night I found him up to something on that two-track above my cabin." I carried the roll over to the counter.

"Ronnie know?" he asked, rising from the stool.

Based upon the young game warden's testimony Horace Baker was convicted of firing a high-powered rifle from the cab of his truck. Baker had mistaken a bunch of decoys for a flock of geese, wounding a man who had been hiding among the decoys while hunting with friends. His two-year jail sentence was unusually long, making front-page news in the *Sun Journal* and *Bangor Daily News*, with even the *Portland Press Herald* carrying the story.

I shook my head. "Haven't had the chance to speak with him. Thought it better to provide the news in person." I passed the roll across the counter. "How 'bout a ham-and-cheese sandwich for the road?"

"Where's that hard-headed dog of yours?" Jeff asked as he pulled a long knife from under the counter and sliced the roll in two halves.

"Left him back in town. He's getting too old to spend every day out on the water." My hip ached from sitting in the boat all afternoon and after a moment I added, "Come to think of it, so am I."

Limping over to an old red freezer, I unlatched the top and pulled out a cold bottle of root beer from between the ice.

The storeowner chuckled. "Mayo?" he asked, crossing over to a small metal container that held cold cuts.

"Mustard," I replied. "Doctor says I should cut down on my dairy."

Chapter Thirteen

"You think the fish'll still be biting, Mr. D'Amico?"

I was seated beside J.J. Ross and his father, our legs dangling from the open tailgate of the mechanic's pickup. We'd been waiting for Sam Treadwell for more than twenty minutes, the three of us listening to songbirds in the waning light.

"Look over there." Junior pointed to the tree where the sign for the road beside the Cupsuptic River had been nailed.

When not working at the garage or helping Fin MacDougall cut and deliver firewood, Wayne Ross could be found harvesting fish and game from the forest that surrounded the town, his love of fishing only surpassed by his passion for hunting grouse. Those of us dependent on him to keep our machinery running and vehicles on the road knew there would be little service during those days in May, when the big fish chase the smelt up the rivers, and again during early October, when the young mechanic, accompanied by his Brittany spaniel, spent his days stalking the stands of spruce for grouse.

"I betcha The Bear did it." J.J.'s eyes went wide.

I hopped off the tailgate and walked closer to the tree to get a better look. Sure enough, there was a set of claw marks embedded in the trunk where the sign should have been. When I sat back down beside him, the younger Ross asked, "You sure they'll be biting?"

Junior read everything he could on the subject of fishing, and although the level of the mechanic's skill left something to be desired, it did not dampen his enthusiasm. His son, who had turned ten last fall, accompanied his father whenever his mother would allow.

"A nice night like this with no breeze, they'll be dimpling the surface until dark," I assured the boy.

We were parked just above the top of the Morton Cutoff Road, along the edge of the two-track that winds through the forest on the east side of the Cupsuptic River. It was uncommonly warm for the last week in May and Wayne broke out bottles of root beer from a Styrofoam cooler. We took long, lazy pulls while he and I swapped fish stories to the delight of his son. I still hadn't hooked up with Ronnie Adams, the warden spending his time trying to track down whatever or whoever was pulling down signs along logging roads from Wentworth Location to Eustis.

We heard Sam's vehicle before we saw it. Dust settled around the back of his blue-and-white Bronco as it careened to a halt.

"Sorry," the veterinarian groaned from the open window.

"You're nearly an hour late." Junior looked down at his watch as I crossed to the back of the big SUV and began loading our gear inside.

"Donnie Johnson came by just as I was closing up. His Jack impaled himself on a stick and I had to stitch him up before leaving."

"He okay?" I asked while securing Wayne's cooler between our fishing rods and canoe paddles. Walking around to the front of the Bronco, I slid into the passenger seat beside Sam. The veterinarian had flung a flannel shirt over his light blue scrubs, but otherwise had not changed out of his office attire.

"He'll be fine. Needed a few stitches and a shot of penicillin, but it'll take more than a punctured belly to keep a Jack Russell down."

After father and son climbed into the back, Sam sped up the road, dust rising in a gray cloud behind us. Ten minutes later, we passed Big Boy Falls.

"Did you notice the mile markers are all down?" he said to no one in particular.

Wayne grunted from the backseat, his eyes focused on a box of flies he had opened, his mind occupied with which pattern to start off the evening.

"It's The Bear," his son yelled from beside his father.

A mile or so up the road we stopped short to prevent hitting a hare, watching as it hopped wildly for a few yards before darting into the forest. After a while Sam again applied the brakes, this time to allow a young moose to trot across the road. After another twenty minutes, we came upon two dilapidated snowmobile bridges, one a few yards up the two-track from the other. After crossing over them, we drove alongside the Canyon, a section of stream with a number of picturesque waterfalls, and one of my favorite haunts on our side of the Milky Way.

Dusk had descended over the forest, and we considered stopping short of our intended destination to fish the stream above the bridges, but after a brief discussion, we pushed on, Sam pointing to the tree where the Wiggle Brook Road sign had been removed. Turning left, we drove for another mile or so, making a right and passing over another, smaller bridge onto a narrower two-track where saplings scraped either side of the Bronco. Less than a mile from the Canadian border, the dirt road narrowed into an alder-choked trail with tall grass growing across it. The veterinarian pulled to a halt in a small clearing between the end of the road and the little-used trail. On one side of the clearing, a well-trodden path led to our intended destination.

"We'd better get a move on if we want to catch the end of the evening hatch," Junior warned. His son, unable to contain his excitement, raced down to the water.

Held in the palm of spruce-covered hills, Cupsuptic Pond is, at its deepest, only a few feet, the edges of its tea-colored waters surrounded by low-growing blueberry bushes. Roughly oval in shape, the source of the Cupsuptic River is more of a bog, accessed by a single muddy path pocked by the hooves of moose.

I had hoped J.J. would have the chance to see the pond's gold-and-orange hues as the sun slowly set, but we had arrived too late. Even so, there was still time for the youngster to play tag with a few of the pond's resident brook trout.

The three of us followed the boy, slogging single file down the narrow trail, our boots making squishy sounds in the mud. We carried our rods pointing backward, stopping at the water's edge. At first glance, it appeared to be drizzling, the pond's surface disturbed by a plethora of tiny ringlets, but as the first stars appeared in a cloudless sky, I knew that below each set of rings there was a tiny trout feeding on the final stage of that evening's hatch of insects. I couldn't think of a better way to spend a Friday evening in May. In a couple of weeks, black flies would make it nearly impossible to fish at dusk. A few weeks after that, mosquitoes and no-see-ums would join in the bloodlust, but tonight there wasn't a hint of the horde of bloodsucking insects that would plague the backwoods for most of June.

There was no room for a back cast, the balsam and spruce stretching their branches out above the low-growing blueberries that ringed the edge of the pond. When J.J. tried to bully his way through the bushes, I motioned to Junior, father pulling his son backward, knowing that the pond's bottom could suck a man down like quicksand.

Turning back toward the trail, I pulled a few balsam branches off the small canoe that Sam kept chained to a tree. We had intended to take turns, two at a time, but with the shadows growing longer, I looked over at the veterinarian, who shrugged his shoulders, knowing that there was no more than thirty minutes remaining before it would grow too dark to see. As he helped J.J. into the bow, I handed Junior the paddles we had brought with us, giving the canoe a shove toward the center of the pond.

While the vet found a nearby boulder to sit on, I waited for the first whoop before heading back up to the clearing. Although uncertain as to whether father or son had hooked a fish, trudging up to the Bronco, I was confident they would have much to talk about on the drive back to town.

With its window down, I was able to swing open the SUV's tailgate and grab a bottle of root beer from the cooler inside. Leaning against the vehicle's fender, I looked up at the darkening sky while taking a long pull. I located first one and then the other stars comprising the handle of the Big Dipper.

Although I had no idea what was ailing Bailey, and didn't like the idea of finding an infamous poacher between my camp and Hollyhock Leventhal's dig site, at least Rusty had earned some extra fees guiding my sports. Combined with what money the film crew spent in their store, the Millers might yet make it out of the financial hole they found themselves in. Whether or not God was up there somewhere, down here, at least for the moment, all appeared not so bad with my world.

Taking another pull from the cold bottle of pop, I traced an imaginary line from the Dipper's bottom two stars to Polaris, and from the North Star, down the Little Dipper's handle. While searching for Cassiopeia, the constellation that appears in the northern sky as a drunken W, I heard the sound of a vehicle coming up the road before seeing its headlights.

There are few anglers willing to make the trip to fish for palm-size trout and these days the path leading to the border is rarely traveled, most in town not aware of its existence. Richard Morrell once told me that while in high school, he used the now overgrown trail to score pot in Canada, where it was easier to purchase, and a retired warden I know remembers French Canadians traveling down the well-worn path to poach moose and deer.

Back then, there was no effective force to guard the border between western Maine and Canada. No longer as popular as they had once been, since 9/11, when the Border Patrol opened its Rangeley station, trails like the one above the pond are now routinely checked. It was for this reason that I expected Bobby Mendez, or one of the other border patrol agents, to pull next to the Bronco. Instead, a Chevy Silverado turned astride Sam's vehicle. Although dusty, the black paint of the American-made pickup looked new. The truck was tricked out with a set of lights above the cab and a brush guard bolted to the front of the hood. A tarp covered the bed.

Living in a small town, you get to know your neighbors' vehicles, but I couldn't recall anyone who drove such a fancy vehicle. Besides, no one I knew could afford something so expensive, except Joe Hawley, and he drove a Humvee. So, when the driver pressed a button lowering the truck's window, I was surprised to find Arthur Wentworth, Sr. at the wheel.

"Nice rig," I said, still leaning against the back of the Bronco.

Drawing on his cigarette, the other man squinted through the smoke that circled around the cab's expansive interior, the toxic gray cloud slipping out the partially opened window.

"Thought I'd try my luck, but seems you beat me to it." Even in the uncertain light, I could make out the decrepit state of the man's teeth. The elder Wentworth's nervous grin reminded me of a dog after he's licked a toad.

Looking over my shoulder, Arthur, Sr. stared up the alder-choked trail and then down the path to the pond. Tossing his cigarette out the window, he grunted something about seeing me on the flip side while slowly backing the truck out from beside Sam's vehicle. I watched him watch me through the Silverado's rearview mirror as he drove back in the direction he came. Searching the ground, I found the cigarette butt and crushed it with the tip of my boot. Certain that it was now out, I grabbed a flashlight from the glove compartment of the Bronco and followed its beam down to the pond, where Junior was helping Sam chain the canoe to a tree.

Chapter Fourteen

How Arthur Wentworth, Sr. had come to be driving an expensive truck was one more of life's many riddles, no less a puzzlement than Horace Baker showing up on the road above my camp. After Sam dropped me off, I drove into town to pick up Buck, who had spent the day lazing around Bailey's apartment. I figured he'd be up for a day on the water. Besides, I was hoping Bailey might open up about what was bothering her. Instead, after trudging up the stairs to her apartment, I found a note on the kitchen table telling me she had gone out with Jeanne and Martha Dudley.

Call me a coward, but I felt relieved. I've always tried to avoid confrontation, not necessarily a good trait, and more than likely the reason why my relationship with my daughter remained tenuous. Although knowing it would be better to clear the air, I scribbled a few words in response to Bailey's note, added an *I Love You*, and headed back to camp. On the way to the cabin, I told myself that this was preferable to waking early the next morning and making the long drive to the lake to meet Magalini.

After spending the remainder of the evening preparing lunch for my second excursion with the director, I found sleep impossible as worry swirled in and out of my head. Waking early, I walked down the path from my cabin to Hollyhock Leventhal's campsite while it was still dark. Surprised to find that she was not there, I hiked back to the cabin, where Buck was waiting beside the truck.

Pulling into the dirt lot at the bottom of Aziscohos Lake, I forced my concerns to the back of my mind while focusing on the task at hand. With Buck sitting beside me, and the Grumman strapped to its trailer, I stopped the faded orange pickup in front of the Lafleurs' general store.

With an average depth of only thirty feet and an easy swim from one side of the lake to the other, Aziscohos is both shallow and narrow by comparison with the lakes to the east. Although its lack of depth produces smaller salmon than those found in the deeper lakes of the region, these traits give the water a more intimate feel. Less built up than Rangeley Lake or Hawley Pond, the few camps along its eastern shoreline do without utility or phone lines. Tom Rider's fishing lodge is the only improvement along its western shoreline, with the Lafleurs' campgrounds tucked into the southeastern end.

Bruno Magalini tapped his boot on the heavy slab of slate outside the store's front door, a long brown cigarette dangling from the corner of his mouth. LeBron Hayes stood behind him, a silver thermos in his large hand, the shiny SUV parked beside them. It was a bit after six in the morning, and although it was the last day of the last full week of May, the temperature overnight had fallen into the low forties, making the fog coming off the lake quite thick. Buck looked out the open window, sniffing the scents that rode upon the cold mist.

A swirl of heat rose from the thermos as LeBron screwed off the top and poured coffee into a cup, handing it to Magalini, who scowled in my direction. Placing the thermos on the hood of the Tahoe, the former fullback leaned into the back door of the large vehicle, coming back out with his employer's rod tube and daypack. He strode over to my truck as I opened the door and climbed out.

"Mr. Magalini rarely rises before eleven," he cautioned while helping me arrange the gear in the bed of the Toyota, "and he's still pissed about that fish you put back."

We left LeBron standing by the SUV and pulled up the logging road, the Great Magalini cursing as we bounced along the eastern side of the lake, twice spilling coffee onto his lap as he tried to ignore the big black animal sitting between us. Buck paid little attention to the passenger seated on his right, laying his head on my lap, his rump pressing into the director's side. I stayed on the Lincoln Pond Road for a few miles, turning onto Deer Mountain Road, where I noticed that the signs marking each mile had been torn down. *Busy Bear*, I thought.

The springs of the old vehicle had long since lost their elasticity, the director groaning each time the truck hit a pothole or rumbled over a culvert. Thirty-five minutes later, we drove over the four planks of wood that span Twin Brook, a few moments afterward chugging down the dirt boat ramp near the top of the lake, where the mileage markers had not been disturbed.

The Magalloway Rivers, Big and Little, fall down out of Canada, slipping past the Maine border and flowing through the Parmachenee tract that is comprised of wild timberland surrounding the lake named for the Native American princess through whom Richard Morrell claimed his right of ownership to the surrounding wilderness.

The Big Magalloway slides out of Parmachenee Lake, forming a series of fast rapids interspersed with shallow riffles that sweep over boulders and slippery rocks until emptying into a large pool under the Camp Ten Bridge. Downstream, the river separates into three distinct runs before swinging to the west, where all three come together again to form a wide, slow-moving channel. A Fly-Fishing Only sign posted within sight of Tom Rider's lodge serves as the demarcation between river and Lake. The boat ramp I had pulled down was on the river, not far above this sign.

I guided the trailer down the ramp while the director continued his complaint from the previous outing. As he bemoaned the release of the salmon, cedar waxwings chattered in the trees above us. Leaning out the window, I stopped to watch one of the birds sweep over the surface of the river and catch an insect on the wing. Walking down to the water's edge, I removed the straps holding the Grumman to the trailer. Following a few steps behind, the director embarked on a new tirade, insisting that he use his own rod rather than troll with one of mine. He appeared satisfied when I promised that there would be plenty of time to cast his flies once we reached Camp Ten Bridge, but glared defiantly when I added that until then, the trolling rods would be our best bet. The man had become accustomed to getting his way.

Buck sensed the sport's displeasure and sauntered down the shoreline, zigzagging out of sight on the trail of some mink or otter. Only after I loaded our equipment onto the boat and helped Magalini into the bow did the big dog once again appear at my side. While raising the Lab's hind legs over the Grumman's gunwale, I heard a sound coming from the road. Walking back up the ramp, I noticed that a mileage marker had been torn down and in its place was nailed a hand-painted sign that could have been written by a child, *or perhaps an especially literate bear*, I thought.

The sign read: **HEM-A-ROID HY-WAY**. Another mystery added to my ever-growing list.

When I returned, Buck had curled around my duffel in the center of the boat. As I pushed off, the sound of the outboard reverberated through the mist. By the time we passed the Fly-Fishing Only sign, I'd decided to use the fee the director had promised me to bring the Millers' loan current.

While swinging out into the lake and around the east side of a large island, I added up the numbers a second time just to be sure. Depending upon the tip, there might be enough left over to purchase a used, but exceedingly sweet, bamboo rod displayed in the window of Sun Valley Sports, a fly-fishing shop not far from the Bethel Inn, where Bailey and I spent a February weekend cross-country skiing.

Navigating through a shallow channel and around the other side of the island, I slowed the outboard as we approached a heron rookery. Through the breaking fog we could make out fifty or more of the tall gray birds, each standing precariously on the tippy-tops of spruces, many with heads lowered under their enormous wings, a few staring down at us like gargoyles along a castle wall. A pair glided silently through the fog, their wings extended on either side, looking every bit like two pterodactyls from prehistoric times. Magalini's mood had grown less severe, although the maestro now complained about the moisture in the air, worried that it might damage his expensive camera.

After we passed the herons, I motored into a cove along the opposite shoreline, cutting the engine to allow the director to photograph a bull, the big male raising its head from the shallows, the moose's antlers covered in velvet. Farther up the lake, we encountered a family of otters playing around a partially submerged boulder that Magalini also captured with his camera. Buck, who'd fallen asleep moments after hopping into the boat, failed to raise his head or open an eye.

A few minutes later, we cruised alongside another island, this one opposite Tom Rider's sporting camp and where the previous summer Tom and I had helped a state biologist band two eagle chicks. I once again cut the engine while drawing Magalini's attention to a large nest near the top of a tall spruce. Although there was no movement in the massive labyrinth of branches, a few yards away, in another spruce, a mature eagle, its white head visible through the parting mist, glared down at us from a cold yellow eye as the click of the director's camera reverberated across the still surface of the lake.

Beaver Den Camps consists of a few cabins spread along the lake's western shoreline on either side of a main lodge where sports are able to take their meals. As we drew closer, wisps of fog swirled off the top of the lake like tiny waterspouts rising off the ocean's surface. There were only two vehicles parked beside the cabins and most of Tom's fleet of sixteen-foot Lunds remained tethered to his dock. Business was clearly off.

Proceeding north up the western arm of the lake, I steered the Grumman through a shallow channel and into Sunday Pond, a quiet backwater that contains abundant wildlife. In one of its coves, we spooked a few black ducks nestled among the reeds. In another, we watched three cows grazing lazily on vegetation submerged in water that would dry up by summer. A pair of loons dipped under the surface as we crossed toward the far side of the pond, where springtime warblers chattered amicably along the spruce-lined shore.

The fog began to dissipate, the sun rising higher in the sky as I motored out the other side, passing by the boat ramp where earlier we had put in. Turning up the eastern arm of the lake, I spotted a boil fifty or so feet off our bow. A moment later a set of rings rippled outward when the nose of a large salmon broke through the surface. I told Magalini to put aside his camera while handing him one of the trolling rods. For the next hour we swung over some of my favorite holes, cruising past tributaries where salmon liked to congregate to feed on smelt. Although we took a few fish, none were worth photographing, and Magalini soon became impatient.

Stripping off my fleece jacket, I rolled up the sleeves of my flannel shirt and leaned back against the outboard. As the Grumman worked against the river's sluggish current, my thoughts meandered from an educated bear to a notorious poacher. At least I had solved one problem: My plan to bail out the Millers was sound. Magalini's generous fee would bring their loan current with enough left over to pay for the little cane rod I coveted.

My thoughts gradually turned to Bailey. Especially sensitive because of the difference in our ages, I could not help but wonder if perhaps she had lost interest in me.

Then there was Danni Donovan. Why hadn't I told Bailey about her? Was it really because I hadn't had the time? I had to admit the reporter had remained in my thoughts, although just under the surface like a sleek trout feeding in the shadows, rising every so often when you least expect it. Like now, as I leaned back against the outboard, motoring slowly along the spruce-and-balsam shoreline, the sun on my face. What was it about the woman? We had nothing in common, and yet.

"What's that?"

The director's question brought me back to the river. Stopping beside a jumble of limbs and branches, I explained how beavers dragged the wood down to the bank to form their den. While pointing to teeth marks that girdled the trunks of a number of poplar trees, I noticed movement among a stand of spruce between the road and the lake. A moment later a black bear climbed onto a massive boulder. At first the animal stood erect, its arms at its sides, acting more like a human than a bruin as it stared back at me, but then it climbed down and faded into the shadows. *Curious*, I thought.

Pulling on the outboard's cord, I once again engaged the engine. As we turned up a bend in the river the current grew faster, the water level lower than it had been at the beginning of the month, but still high enough to hold some good fish. I dragged the Grumman onto a narrow spit of land and swung a rope around an ancient stump, securing the shallow-draft craft on a cobble shoal. After helping the director to shore, I leaned in to give Buck a hand. Once on land, the old dog ignored us, poking around the stones while engaging in one of his favorite pastimes, nosing at bird guano.

Magalini's mood brightened when I handed him the leather case that held his fly rod. The little Thomas and Thomas graphite job that he slid from the sleeve looked expensive. Though short of six feet, the rod's length was perfectly proportioned to its owner's size, and I assumed it was custom built.

I pulled an old Sucrets tin from my breast pocket. Opening the pillbox, I stared down at a blurry assortment of flies. After I replaced my sunglasses with a pair of cheaters, the patterns in the tiny compartment came into focus.

Once the water lowers from its ice-out high, I prefer wet flies to streamers, unless the situation specifically calls for a particular dry fly. The previous winter I had re-read Thomas Pritt's *North Country Flies* and Edmonds and Lee's *North Country Methods*. After these British classics, I finished all three of Sylvester

Nemes' books on soft-hackled flies, dusting off James Leisenrings' two little volumes before Valentine's Day and completing my education with Dave Hughes' informative book on the subject. By opening day, I was thoroughly immersed in the wet-fly culture, especially soft-hackled patterns. So, although at one time my pattern of choice had been the Gold-Ribbed Hare's Ear, I ignored the dozen or more of the fixed-wing flies and decided upon a Pheasant Tail and a Partridge-and-Orange. Stringing one traditional soft-hackle to the other, I was confident that they would produce fish for the demanding Magalini.

Walking my sport around a bend in the river, I pointed out the likely lies in the deep pool below the Camp Ten Bridge. Buck had followed, sniffing out the enticing scents splattered by birds along the streamside stones.

I held my sport's rod while he unlaced his knee-high boots and replaced them with what looked like a child's pair of chest waders that had also been custom made to fit his short legs. Without waiting for additional instruction, the director waded out into the current and climbed onto a boulder. With the wide brim of his black fedora sweeping down over his bad eye and one of his long brown cigarettes clutched between his teeth, the little man cocked his rod back, then forward, repeating this motion twice more before swinging out sixty feet of line in an elegant arc over the wide pool. The wet flies sunk into the fast water along the edge of the far bank as the Great Magalini mended his line to prevent drag. His arms might have been shorter than those of my other sports, but the maestro was as adept at casting a fly line as he was at directing a movie.

On his second drift, the little rod arched forward, Magalini grunting as a brookie powered toward the head of the pool. After releasing the small fish, he lit the cigarette clenched between his teeth, the smell of the smoke mingling with the scent of balsam that drifted out from the surrounding forest.

With the director into his second fish, I looked toward the north, where clouds were building. Buck had sprawled across some tall grass, his eyes closed, the sun warming his side. Trudging downriver, I passed the wide set of riffles that broke around the little island where the Grumman remained tethered.

Carrying my rucksack from the boat, I lay a blanket over a plastic tarp, and began setting out lunch. After cutting a wedge of sharp-tasting pecorino Romano cheese, I placed it on a plate, adding chunks of provolone and soft mozzarella beside slices of ham, salami, pepperoni and capicola. On another plate, I wrapped prosciutto around wedges of melon that had been packed on ice. Looking once more toward the north, I hoped we'd have time for the antipasto before the rain began.

I popped the lid off another container and added pieces of cold chicken marinated in my own spicy Italian red sauce, and after uncorking a bottle of Merlot that Ollie Stubbs had recommended, removed a loaf of crisp Italian bread from an airtight bag. Satisfied that all was in order, my thoughts drifted back to The Bear and then to Horace Baker.

I needed to talk to Ronnie. What was Horace doing between my cabin and Hollyhock Leventhal's dig? I had hoped to find the paleontologist sipping tea upon my return from Cupsuptic Pond, but she was not at her campsite when I walked over to Otter Brook earlier in the morning. Although I figured she'd probably stayed overnight with some friends in town, the thought of Baker showing up well after dark, in the rain, and so close to her camp remained unsettling. I had replayed the night a number of times, but with no good endings. Then there was The Bear. I was ruminating on the wonderment of an animal smart enough to systematically tear down signs and replace them with those of his own when a series of barks drew my attention upriver.

Since his injury, Buck would bark for no apparent reason, sometimes raising his head from sleep to let out a long blood-curdling call; other times howling while staring off into the distance as if gazing into his future. Even Rose, always up for an adventure, had begun to ignore the old dog's increasing eccentricities. It was for this reason that I failed to heed his warning—that is, until I saw Magalini's wide-brimmed fedora floating past the Grumman.

In my haste to race up the stony shoreline, I tripped, tumbling forward, the right side of my face bouncing off a boulder, my elbow jammed between the cobble. Ignoring the pain, I came around the bend to find Buck standing in water up to his chest. The big dog stared first in my direction and then toward the turbulent current where the tip of the director's little graphite rod protruded from the surface a foot or so beyond the large boulder where I had left him. The tip of the rod that rose above the river arched forward, a taut fly line extending downstream.

Behind the rod an undulating patch of golden weed swayed just beneath the surface, but then the weed rose, and with it the head of Bruno Magalini, water sputtering from his mouth as he took a deep breath. Before I could move, he once more sank from sight, his blond hair waving just under the surface.

With the river's current pushing hard against my calves, I crab-walked past the boulder. I could see Magalini holding his breath, his arms raised above his head, the butt of the little graphite rod clasped tightly in his pudgy hands, the tip pulsating with life as a fish struggled to break free in the rapids beyond the pool. The current swirled around my chest as I locked my arms around the waterlogged sport, dragging him kicking and sputtering toward shore.

Expletives echoed under the clouds that had closed upon the river as the little man lay panting upon the guano-stained bank. I thought I might vomit from the pain. Looking down, I saw that the Great Magalini's fly rod no longer throbbed, the line as limp as the long brown cigarette that still hung from his trembling lips.

Chapter Fifteen

There is always the danger of hypothermia, even in springtime, and when my sport's teeth began to chatter I thought it prudent to strip him out of his wet clothes. Heading back without eating our lunch, I stopped only to pack the food, collecting the director's boots from along the shoreline and his hat from the branch of a sweeper as we motored along with the slow-moving current. Down to his bright red socks and black silk boxers, the Great Magalini sat hunched in the Grumman's bow while huddled under the green blanket I'd previously spread out for our streamside lunch. With the soggy fedora draped down upon his head, he grasped the bottle of Merlot while taking long chugs of wine between bites of a chicken leg. His eyes flashed anger whenever catching sight of mine.

The scrapes on my palms were minor, and although my elbow still hurt, it was the gash on my face that concerned me. The flesh around the wound quickly swelled, blurring the vision of my right eye.

"I could've taken that fish if you had only minded your own business." The Great Magalini tossed the chicken leg over the side. Reaching over Buck's inert body, he tore off a chunk of the Italian bread and grabbed a wedge of pecorino cheese. Buck remained curled among the gear in the middle of the boat, and although the dog hadn't moved since we'd pushed off the shoal, he eyed the food each time Magalini reached across him. The maestro could have drowned had the current swept him downriver, but I said nothing as he ranted on about my incompetence.

Raindrops sprinkled down as I steered along the eastern shoreline. Not far into the lake and a few hundred yards above the little rivulet known as Hurricane Brook we came upon Merle Lansing's cabin, where I knew we could hole up should the storm catch us.

I always pack rain gear because of the unpredictability of the weather and was contemplating breaking it out when a Rangeley boat, its wooden hull painted traditional gray, motored across the mouth of the cove that curves around the outlet of the brook. Two sports trolled lines from either side of the sturdy craft, their guide sitting in the stern while working the outboard. The bill of a cap was pulled down tight over his eyes.

Drawing closer, I saw that the sports were women, each exceptionally attractive. Looking up from under his cap was Rusty Miller, a guilty smile spread across his face. A week's worth of orange stubble framed the familiar moustache that hid his upper lip.

The women's jeans appeared painted to their figures, designer types, not like the kind I wear, neither loose, frayed nor stained. I recognized the one in the bow. She had accompanied the guy who had pushed aside Danni Donovan and her cameraman. As we drew closer I studied the woman's features. Long black hair fell down to her shoulders with bangs cut in a straight line just above her eyes. Tall and slim, she appeared fit, and although in her twenties, could be mistaken for a young teen. Her friend looked older, somewhere north of thirty, with the type of body that had made Hugh Hefner a wealthy man. She wore her red hair in a ponytail.

Rising unsteadily to her feet, the woman sitting amidships waved her arms over her head while calling out, "Bruno!"

"Mr. Magalini," the other hailed from the Rangeley's bow.

"Sit down!" growled Rusty, his sports giggling like schoolgirls as the shorter one fell backward onto the boat's wooden seat.

Gathering the blanket around him, Magalini nodded in their direction.

"Natalie, Gina," he called out.

I looked over at my sport.

"Natalie Jennings and Gina Summers," he said, as if their names alone should be sufficient to identify the two women.

I cut the Grumman's engine, Rusty doing the same with his outboard, the two of us grabbing the railing of each other's craft, the Grumman floating between the Rangeley and the near shoreline of the lake, the two boats bobbing side by side, our bow to their stern.

"Jeanne's guiding your sports while I volunteered to take these fine ladies out." Rusty smirked.

As we floated past the mouth of the cove, I could hear the sound of Hurricane Brook disgorging its springtime current into the lake. A vague scent of balsam drifted out from the surrounding forest, hanging above us in air that had become heavy while rain periodically spit down from the dark clouds overhead. A raven called, and a few moments later a second bird responded, their hoarse cries carrying across the water.

"What happened to you?" Rusty pointed to my face. My cheek stung when I touched it, my fingers coming away with a trace of blood. "And him?" The guide's bloodshot eyes turned toward the director.

Before I could answer, the Great Magalini rose to recount his tale. Words streamed from his lips as rapidly as the current pouring forth from the nearby brook. The maestro described his cast and how the fish, striking hard, powered straight upriver, stopping in the deepest part of the pool, just under the bridge. The guy was an artist, knowing how to paint his tale with broad strokes, adding detail to bring the story to life. With one hand holding the blanket at his waist, the director used his free hand to push up the brim of the river-soaked fedora.

"Biggest fish I ever hooked," he lamented. "I pumped the damn rod, but instead of bringing the bastard to shore, it turned him downriver."

Flourishing the wide-brimmed hat above his head, my sport modulated his voice from a deep baritone to a whisper as we climbed with him down off the large boulder, the sun breaking out from behind a cloud, its light in our eyes, warming our faces, the trout fighting downstream, the sound of the reel whirling in our ears. We slipped into the treacherous current as the fish made another run, followed him step by step until losing our footing and going under while the mighty trout thrashed about in the rough water below the pool.

Rusty's sports had laid down their rods, leaning forward to hear what happened next and adding a few oohs and ahhs whenever they deemed the story warranted it. Like Cato arguing his case before the Roman Senate, Magalini held the blanket as if it were a toga. While standing, knee bent, red sock on the bow of the Grumman, the director explained how he intended to walk only a foot or two into the river in his effort to subdue the fish. Unaware that the Magalloway's cobble can be slippery, the river bottom pocked with holes of varying size, he demonstrated how he lost his footing while nearly falling off the side of the Grumman.

Magalini punctuated his oratory with grand gestures, his movements becoming more frenetic as the tale progressed, the women enthralled with the performance. Having heard my share of fish stories, and told a few of my own, my attention momentarily turned toward Rusty, who had removed a canteen from his pack. After taking a long pull, he screwed the cap back on, shrugging his shoulders in response to my frown.

Although the Grumman is a steady craft, I asked the director to sit down, but the maestro would not be denied his dramatic finale. My sport described holding his breath, and while unable to gain purchase, rising for air, each time sliding back down into the deep water as he held tight to the little Thomas and Thomas rod.

"Lucky you didn't drown your sorry ass." Rusty had taken another long pull from his canteen. Although addressing my sport, the guide directed his eyes at me. We both knew a drowned client would not be good for business. *Nor would a drunk guide*, I thought.

"Yes, well, I had that fish tired out. Would have taken him too, if it weren't for his incompetence." Magalini pointed an accusing finger in my direction.

"Natalie!" Rusty, who had been sitting with his back against the Rangeley's outboard, pointed over the director's shoulder into the cove. Following his gaze, we watched a wake break across the lake's surface ten feet or so beyond the Grumman, heading toward the outlet of Hurricane Brook. The younger actress grabbed her rod from the Rangeley's bow, checking the reel with her thumb. The line, taut as piano wire, crossed over the Grumman's gunwale. I held the aluminum craft against Rusty's wooden Rangeley boat while ignoring the sting to my palms.

"Magnificent!" Magalini cried. The director was leaning over the Grumman's bow while pointing toward a huge salmon that had exploded into the air, its tail skimming across the lake before disappearing under the surface. My sport had barely uttered the word when the fish sounded a second time, leaping skyward, its tail clearing the lake's surface before falling back down on its side, water splashing outward in all directions. Gina squealed with excitement while Natalie's eyes narrowed with determination.

Maintaining her composure, the younger woman sat in the bow of the Rangeley boat. As she worked the rod from side to side, Rusty provided sparing instruction. The fly line remained stretched above the Grumman and over Buck's inert body, the Labrador oblivious to the excitement created by the fish that was as large as any I'd seen taken from the lake.

My cheek throbbed, my elbow still aching. The sting in my hands had turned to cramps, and Rusty, sensing my discomfort, leaned in, taking a turn at holding the Rangeley and Grumman together. Without saying so, we both worried that the line might snag if the two boats parted.

The empty wine bottle rattled against the Grumman's aluminum bottom as I found my long-handled net. The other guide looked over his shoulder to watch his sport's progress while the rain began to fall harder. Magalini waved me off when I held out a poncho, the maestro engrossed in shouting direction to his starlet. Zipping up my jacket, I crawled over Buck and under the actress's fly line, handing Rusty my long-handled net while once again grabbing the rail of the Rangeley boat.

"I'm gonna slide the Grumman backward. Push your boat forward and if we're lucky, she won't get hung up." Moving one hand over the other, I motioned for Rusty to go to his sport's aid.

The salmon chose that moment to reverse direction, Natalie's line going slack, falling inside our boat and coiling over our gear as the young woman reeled, struggling to keep up with the fish that sped directly toward us.

Buck had raised his head when we'd first entered the cove, lowering it when he recognized Rusty. Snoring through the fish story, the old Lab had failed to stir, even as we shifted our bodies about the boat. I grabbed the fly line where it lay in loose coils around the dog's back and allowed it to peel forth as the fish crossed under the two boats. I let go when the line once again grew taut, cutting against the metal railing of the Grumman. While Natalie's rod extended toward the Grumman and Hurricane Brook, she turned, staring wild-eyed over her shoulder into the open lake where the fish had fled.

It continued raining, causing Rusty to break out foul weather gear on his boat. Although Gina slipped a poncho over her shoulders, Natalie, her attention divided between the fish and her rod, did not dare do the same. The salmon was out there, taking the young actress into her backing that threatened to fray against the railing of the Grumman. Rusty's sport stood in the bow of the Rangeley, her shoulders soaked, rain dropping from her bangs, the long trolling rod pointed in the opposite direction from the fish. Rusty was now huddled by her side while Gina kneeled in the middle of the Rangeley, her hands gripping the side of the Grumman while I held on to her boat.

"Give it to me," I cried to Natalie, knowing that at any moment her line might snap, the rod splinter.

Unwilling to give up the fight, the actress, her eyes pleading, looked toward Rusty, who nodded his agreement. The young woman continued to hesitate, not wanting to give up the fish she fought so hard to bring to the boat, but then bent forward, handing me the rod while a combination of tears and rain streamed down her cheeks.

"Ready?" I yelled to Rusty.

"Ready," hollered the guide, who was hunkered over the far side of the Rangeley. With that, I allowed the butt of the trolling rod to follow the tip into the water, letting go only after the entire rod was submerged and bent under the Grumman's hull.

"Oh no!" Natalie almost leaped into my boat when I let loose, but Rusty had bent forward, his arms stretched out to catch the rod as it slipped under the two boats.

The maneuver might have worked if it wasn't for Magalini. Unaware of our plan, the director jumped from the Grumman into the Rangeley, distracting Rusty, who missed the rod that slipped between his outstretched hands.

One moment my sport stood on the wooden craft's decking, the next, he climbed onto the gunwale, his toes flexed, knees bent. Before either Rusty or I could react, the Great Magalini shed the green blanket, performing a perfectly executed swan dive, suspended above the water, in only his black fedora, black boxers and the bright red socks that stretched to just below his knees, which were the last thing we saw, until moments later, when he reappeared twenty or so feet out into the lake.

The four of us watched the director hang on to the rod as the salmon took him on a Nantucket sleigh ride, Rusty motoring the Rangeley in my wake with the actresses squealing above the sound of the two engines. Even Buck, now roused from his slumber, stood, his front paws on the bow of the Grumman, his ears blowing backward as he howled into the wind. With one hand, the maestro managed to retain the black fedora that he waved above his head while hanging on to the butt of the trolling rod with his other.

Although it felt longer, it took only a minute, perhaps two, to catch up, but when I grabbed my sport by his shorts, the waistband ripped, the director now naked except for his red socks and black hat. While Natalie worked the Rangeley's outboard, Rusty bent over the bow. Holding my long-handled net in both hands, the guide lowered it toward the lake, but just then the salmon decided to go deep.

Cutting our engines, we sat silently and looked for signs of the director.

Seconds later, like Jonah back from the whale, Bruno Magalini bobbed to the surface. While the maestro sputtered and spit, his eyes wide, Rusty slid the net under him. My sport held onto the trolling rod as the women helped haul him into the Rangeley, reeling in the fish that by now was done-in. Gina clapped her hands as the salmon rolled on the surface, Natalie attempting to disguise her disappointment.

Neither Rusty nor I had seen a salmon as large as the one the director had subdued. We worked on the fish for some time. Unable to revive it, Rusty first offered the Leviathan to his sport, but when she declined, Magalini was more than willing to accept the trophy.

On the drive back down the lake, I examined my face in the Toyota's mirror. By then, my right eye had nearly closed as a result of the bluish-green lump that had swelled around the jagged cut across my cheek. Although wet and weary, my sport was in remarkably good spirits by the time we pulled into the parking lot beside the camp store.

LeBron Hayes was waiting, the former pro athlete raising an umbrella over the passenger door of my truck. I shrugged my shoulders when the big man stared from my face to his employer, who had remained bundled in the wool blanket.

After seeing the director off, I drove toward my cabin, the Toyota's lights cutting through the rain that had not abated. Turning up the heat, my thoughts first turned toward Bailey, in whose lap I would have liked to lay my aching face. But as the wipers beat time, it was Danni Donovan's thick black hair and piercing blue eyes that came to mind as I caught myself humming "Galway Girl."

Chapter Sixteen

I hadn't seen Hollyhock Leventhal since the afternoon when we watched the deer give birth to twins. The first season she began her dig, Hollyhock would walk the short distance from her camp to my cabin, sometimes to borrow a tool, more often to drink a beer or share a meal together, occasionally just to chat. This had continued over the years, and I had become accustomed to seeing her at least once a week. If I were out, she would let herself in like she had the other night, leaving a note with one of those silly smiley faces drawn under her name.

With my concern for Holly mounting, I decided to walk over to Otter Brook even though every part of my body ached with pain. After feeding Buck an early dinner, I raised the hood of my poncho and plodded over to the stream, but still no Holly. There wasn't anything to do in the rain, and I tramped back up the path, intending to return in the morning for a better look around.

Back in the cabin, I examined the egg-sized bump in the bathroom mirror. Rinsing a washcloth with warm water, I dabbed gingerly along the apex of the swelling and then cleaned the scrapes on my palms. I looked through the cabinet over the sink, grabbing a tube that contained ointment meant to prevent infection and applied it to the cuts and bruises, taping a bandage over my elbow. There wasn't much else to do except swallow my usual dose of ibuprofen.

When I woke the next morning, my entire body felt like I'd played four quarters opposite LeBron Hayes. With the sky now blue and the sun still behind the hills to the east of my cabin, I dragged myself out from under the covers. After a hot shower and a mug of tea, I tramped over to Holly's dig. Everything looked neat and in order, but no paleontologist. I hiked down to the road, but Holly's van was not where she usually parked it, in the logger's depot above the culvert and a few yards up the road from where Horace Baker's truck had been parked. There was nothing to indicate a problem. The paleontologist could have been spending a few days with friends or perhaps she flew back to the Midwest. So why did I feel so uneasy?

I had left Buck sleeping on the porch, but upon my return found him off on one of his walkabouts. An interesting sport had booked time with me for that afternoon, but afterward, I'd be meeting Ronnie Adams and some of the other guys for our monthly "boys' night out." I hoped the warden would know what to do.

When the dog failed to appear, I left a bowl of food on the porch and returned Rocky to his box on the shelf of my bedroom closet. Driving toward Richardson Lake, I slipped an early Van Morrison disc into the CD player and listened to the Belfast Cowboy's "Stoned Me."

The man waiting beside the public boat launch did not look like the Catholic priest who had approached me a few days earlier while I was having lunch at the Wooden Nickel. This morning he wore chest waders over a gray flannel shirt rather than black pants and jacket, a jolly, red-paisley neckerchief replacing the plain white collar he had been wearing when I met him at the roadhouse. His skin was darker than my darkest tan after a season on the water. As I rolled down the window of the truck, Father Brendan raised his polarized glasses to the top of his head and extended his arm in my direction.

"Sal-va-torrrre." He pronounced my name in the same singsong manner as Holly used when she spoke. "I hope the other bloke got as good as he gave," the priest said when he saw my face.

"One of those cases of an irresistible force meeting an immovable object." I was unable to place the priest's accent, but it seemed similar to that of the Irish paleontologist.

Backing the Toyota down the cement ramp, I guided the trailer into the water. Removing the straps, I slipped the Grumman into the lake while Father Brendan gathered his pack from the rental car he had parked along the side of the road.

After loading our gear into the aluminum boat, I helped the priest into the bow while taking my place in the stern. A breeze out of the north caused little wavelets to break against the boat's bow as we motored out of the sheltered cove.

"Well, Sal-va-torrrre, on a morning such as this, I am confident the Good Lord is smilin' down upon us. Wouldn't you agree?"

The sun had risen over the rim of hills surrounding the eastern shore of the lake, taking the edge off the early morning chill. I didn't feel like the priest's employer had been paying much attention to yours truly over the last few days. I thought of Hollyhock Leventhal and hoped that whoever was up there might be smiling down on her if not on me. Then there was Bailey. It was the height of fishing season, but I hoped to find time later in the evening to figure things out.

Although happy to be on the water, where life's problems always seemed a bit less pressing, I looked over at the priest and said, "The spirit would like to believe; but it's my flesh that's having its doubts."

When I questioned him about his accent, Father Brendan explained that although born in Nigeria, he had been converted to Christianity by Augustinian Fathers and while still a boy shipped out to Ireland, returning to Africa after attending seminary school.

"It is ironic, is it not, Sal-va-torrrre, that the lack of priests in your country requires this African shepherd to tend to an American flock in much the same way that my order did for the people of Nigeria."

The priest laughed, something he did at the least provocation, while explaining the irony in the name he chose at the time of his ordination.

"Legend has it that Brendan the Navigator lived in the Middle Ages. An Irish monk, he visited America before the Vikings set out on their voyages." Smiling broadly, the younger man said, "Spreading the gospel in much the same way as I do." The Nigerian had the whitest teeth I'd ever seen.

The sun was playing hide-and-seek behind the shifting clouds. As we turned up Richardson Lake we could see Upper Dam looming in the distance, the camps set side-by-side along the north shoreline bathed in light.

When the Nigerian concluded the story of his namesake, I told one of my own, describing the history of the wooden dam that holds back the waters of Mooselookmeguntic Lake from those of Richardson while repeating the story of Carrie and Wallace Stevens.

Throughout the afternoon we switched back and forth from streamers to caddis imitations. Sitting with my back against the outboard, my face to the sun, my thoughts slipped from one to another until fixing once more on Hollyhock Leventhal. I told myself that the professor of paleontology could take care of herself. For all I knew, she had returned to her dig and was mucking 'round in the mud for the bits and bones she found so interesting.

The plan had been to change my clothes and take a quick shower at Bailey's apartment before meeting the gang at Moose Alley, but upon our return to the boat launch, the priest had requested we drive to Upper Dam so he could snap a few photographs of the plaque erected in honor of Carrie Stevens. Although it was too late to stop at Bailey's apartment, I drove directly into Rangeley, hoping to meet her at the bowling alley named after that section of Route 16 known for its moose sightings.

Pulling into the lot, I found a space in back, parked my pickup where the trailer would be out of the way, and walked toward the entrance with the gait of a man feeling his age.

Inside, the sound of balls hitting pins rose from a line of lanes set along the back wall. To the left of the door, Ronnie Adams sat hunched over a hamburger at one of the tables that lined a dance floor below a small bandstand where the night's entertainment was setting up their equipment. My daughter's on-again, off-again boyfriend had grown out the buzz cut he had maintained since high school, his blond hair combed neatly from either side of a razor-straight part. The young warden still wore his uniform, green pants tucked into mud-splashed boots that were laced above his ankles. He hadn't shaved and looked tired.

"The other guy look as bad as you?" he asked as I approached.

"Close encounter of the riverbank kind," I answered.

"You hear from Prudence?" The warden took a bite of burger.

"Me? I'm the last to hear from my daughter. I'd think her boyfriend would have figured that out by now." The question put me in a sour mood.

Ronnie raised a can of cola to his lips as I scanned the room hoping to find Bailey.

"Horace Baker sends his regards. Saw him up the two-track between my cabin and Otter Brook." I stole a French fry from the paper plate in front of him.

"You're worse than your dog." It was his turn to scowl. "Where's the old coot?" The warden looked toward the door.

"Horace?"

"Buck." He frowned. His spring hadn't been much better than my own.

"These days I see him about as much as I see Bailey, but that's another story."

Ronnie leaned back, pushing up the brim of his green cap and closing his eyes. When he opened them again, he said, "I heard Horace was out, but hadn't seen him. Checked his camp, but it was still boarded up."

"Yeah, well, a couple of weeks back, during that heavy rain, I came upon his truck pulled off the two-track just down from my camp."

"Where Otter Brook flows under the road." The warden stated this as a fact rather than a question.

"That's the place. He was coming out of the forest just below the culvert."

I snagged another fry and dragged it through a puddle of ketchup that the warden had squirted onto his plate.

"No law against walking around the woods in the rain."

"Hollyhock Leventhal had set up camp earlier that day. She's starting up another season excavating below the dam at the southern end of the pond. Her tents are pitched just up the brook from where Baker was parked. Took her fishing the next day, but I haven't seen her since, and she wasn't there when I stopped by her camp yesterday morning, last night or this morning."

"She doesn't spend all her waking hours at her camp, does she?"

The warden was right, of course, but I pressed him anyway.

"The same night I bumped into Horace, I found an empty container of worms and the remains of more than two dozen brook trout strewn across the bank below Long Pond, and Jeff Lafleur found the guts of a deer not far from his campsites around the same time."

"Law against that, all right." The warden pushed the plate across the table. He crumpled a napkin over the half-eaten hamburger.

"Oh, and yesterday, I got a glimpse of The Bear. He's not only tearing down signs, but now he's replacing them with those of his own." I described what I had seen the previous morning.

The warden sighed. "Spent one week patrolling around Mooselook and then Upper Richardson Lake, staking out key intersections, and the week after that over to the Kennebago Divide, roughin' it, trying to track down this damn bear everyone's talking about." Ronnie seemed to think for a moment. "Was planning to sleep in tomorrow. You gonna be around later in the afternoon?" He carried his plate to the trash bin.

"I'll be at the cabin until two. After that I'll be on the water till dark."

"That works." The warden paid the waitress. "I'll drop by before you leave."

"Have you seen Bailey?" I asked as we walked toward the counter beside the bowling alley.

"Rusty said something about her feeling under the weather," he replied, grabbing the pair of shoes the pimply-faced kid handed him.

"So, do you guys have any idea who's screwing with the signs?" I found a seat on a bench by the counter.

"As fast as they're replaced, someone's rippin' 'em down." The warden sat beside me.

"The Bear?" I said.

"Like a bear's gonna methodically tear down mileage markers." Ronnie rolled his eyes.

My lower back twinged when I bent down to unlace my boots.

"Would have to be a smart bear, all right," I said, tying the laces of the green-and-white shoes.

Ronnie slid his boots into a compartment under the bench. "At first I thought it was someone who had a grudge against one or another of the paper companies, but we're getting reports on lands owned by all of them."

"Could be one of the old-timers. Figures people should learn how to use a compass. Or maybe some eco-terrorist."

"You have anyone in mind?" He rose from the bench with me a step behind.

"Seems the signs started coming down about the time your friend, Horace, got out of jail."

Ronnie was thinking this over when Danni Donovan walked up arm in arm with Sam Treadwell. I didn't want to admit it, but seeing them together annoyed me. I nodded as they approached.

Danni reached out a hand toward my cheek. While her eyes locked on mine, I explained what had happened. When I joked about her bowling in four-inch heels, she pointed toward a table where the Michael Douglas look-alike was talking with Natalie Jennings. I also recognized LeBron Hayes, Magalini's chauffeur, sitting by himself at a table beside them.

"Turns out, some of the actors have discovered this place," Donovan said. "Thought I might get an interview, but then bumped into your friend, who said you would be dropping by."

The reporter looked terrific in a beige blouse and tan skirt that fell just above her knees. She also looked younger than I remembered, but it might have been her hair, which she had let down.

"And who is this fine officer of the law?" Donovan turned her eyes on Ronnie.

"Woods cop," Ronnie muttered.

Donovan looked back at me.

"He's a game warden, not a police officer," I explained, introducing her to Ronnie as a reporter for the network news.

"Network affiliate," she corrected me.

Sam pointed toward the bar. "You want a beer? We're ordering for everyone."

"Make mine a Long Trail." Ronnie walked toward the lanes.

"I'll take the same," I said, limping after him.

Since the alley opened during the boom years, we had added bowling to our monthly boys' night out. Beldora MacDougall and Karen Ross sat at a table with Donnie Johnson's wife, but I didn't recognize many of the other patrons and assumed they were connected with the movie or had driven up to the popular nightspot from either Bethel or Farmington. Most were jammed around the dance floor, but the lanes were also full. Arthur Wentworth, Sr. slunk past LeBron Hayes' table carrying a longneck. There seemed to be a flicker of recognition in the big man's face, but before I could chew on that bone, Junior Ross waved from one of the lanes.

"Over here," he called.

The mechanic grimaced as I recounted to one and all my fall along the Magalloway.

"Dude." Richard Morrell shook his head from side to side without saying more.

Junior slid down the bench, making room beside Finley MacDougall.

"You're late." Rusty Miller grunted from his seat at the scoring table.

I looked back toward the women. "I don't see Jeanne."

"Spending the night with her mother," he replied.

Magalini had paid me what he'd promised for his two days on the water, including an extravagant tip, but I decided not to reveal my plan to help out the Millers until I could speak with both of them at the same time.

"Did Bailey say what was wrong with her?" I asked the guide.

"Told Jeanne that she might be coming down with a bug and thought a good night's sleep might help. Said to tell you not to worry, she'd see you soon," he replied.

Sitting on a bench behind the adjoining lane, Ollie Stubbs wore an elastic back brace that looked more like a girdle. Arthur Wentworth's son, Arthur, Jr., was crouched low, watching his ball knock down four pins he had missed on his first attempt.

When the young man returned to his seat, Donnie Johnson leaned over to pat him on the back.

"How's Bennie?" I called to Donnie, referring to his Jack Russell.

"Oh, he'll be fine." He let out a nervous chuckle. "Gave me a scare, but Doc put him right."

Sam and Donovan returned with beers for everyone, except Rusty, who had ordered a Jack Daniel's. I wanted to ask Arthur, Jr. about how his father came to be driving the tricked-out Silverado, but Rusty called out, "We gonna yak or bowl?" the guide taking a swallow from his glass before rising to collect his ball.

Ronnie, who had sat down beside me, made room for Donovan, the reporter's skirt riding up her thighs when she squeezed in between us.

"If your fellow officers look as handsome as you, I might have to talk my producer into doing a piece on Maine's Warden Service." The reporter for a network affiliate raised a bottle of Bud Light to her lips, pretending not to notice when the woods cop blushed.

Just then, Rusty's team let out a cry as he bowled a strike. While waiting for his ball to return, the guide swaggered back to the scoring table to take another swig of Jack. On his next turn, he left two pins, but followed that by sweeping them away and adding a spare to his score.

After taking his turn, Ronnie stepped beside Richard Morrell.

"Sup?" Morrell looked up at the warden.

"Any word on Baybrook's suit?" Ronnie asked.

"I expect they'll settle soon enough," the Wabanaki answered.

"Why's that?" The warden had returned to his seat beside Donovan.

Morrell leaned toward him. "If I win, not only do they lose the few acres around my cabin, but all the land north of the lake. The entire Parmachenee tract will be mine. Not sure Baybrook wants to take that chance."

They stared at each other for a moment longer.

"You see anything strange out there?" Ronnie asked.

"Like?" The Native American did not blink.

"Oh, maybe a bear that thinks he's clever, a bear with a grudge against the paper company."

"Not sure what you're getting at, bro." Richard Morrell took a pull on his longneck. "My beef's with Baybrook. I've got nothing against the other paper companies."

"That right?" It was hard to tell if the warden was convinced.

"Just sayin', " Morrell said, as he rose from his seat, walking past the warden to collect his ball.

As the game progressed, Rusty left more and more pins standing, ordering whiskey while the rest of us nursed our beers. Danni Donovan followed me when I walked toward the concession stand to order a sandwich.

"Your friend has a problem," she said, pointing over her shoulder.

"Tell me something I don't know," I muttered.

I looked over at the tables, but LeBron was gone. So was the Michael Douglas look-alike. Scanning the room, I couldn't find Arthur's father, although Natalie remained, a number of men seated around her.

A crowd of young people sat in front of one of the alley's flat-screen TVs, watching a weatherman describe a freak storm that was developing in the Gulf of Mexico. Pushing my way toward the counter, I heard him say that the last time a hurricane hit the East Coast this early in the year was in the late 1800s.

"Hey, Mr. D." Ricky Wilkinson turned from the television and looked in our direction. The twenty-something had briefly dated Fin and Beldora MacDougall's middle daughter before Raisa shipped out to Afghanistan. Tonight he appeared more interested in Donovan, until the girl he was with elbowed him in the ribs.

Slipping her arm around mine, the reporter drew closer to my side.

"I wanted to let you know that Bruno sat down with me for the interview you arranged, and *Hollywood Tonight* has already picked it up and is rushing to get it on the air."

I ordered a grilled cheese sandwich and root beer when the waitress walked over to where we were standing.

"Really, Sal, this could be the break I've been looking for. I'd like to find a way to thank you." The newswoman squeezed my hand. Brushing her lips against my ear, she whispered, "How about dinner?"

Donovan caught me by surprise. I stood staring into those eyes, unable to find any clever words to come to my rescue.

When the girl beside Ricky walked toward the ladies' room, the twenty-something turned back in our direction, asking that I say hello to Raisa for him while once again focusing his attention on the reporter. The young man bore that self-satisfied expression that some youths carry into adulthood, until someone or something wipes it from their face.

The summer before 9/11 I had taken Ricky and Raisa out on Little Kennebago Lake, and although Raisa remained animated throughout the afternoon, Ricky had that same look on his face. It was as if he had seen all life had to offer by the time he was sixteen.

"It's settled, then. Dinner at the Northwoods Inn." She pulled out her smartphone, sliding her finger over the screen. "I'm going to be out of town for the remainder of the week. How about next Friday, say around seven?" The reporter ignored the young man's leer.

When I didn't reply, she persisted.

I was still thinking of a way out when Rusty called from the lanes, "Hey, lover boy, yougonnabowlorwhat?" He was beginning to slur his words.

Chapter Seventeen

I drove west along Route 16, staring up through the open window at the nebulous band of stars that stretched overhead. Normally, I might stop to gaze up at the galaxy that we call home, but it had been another long day on the water that stretched into night while we bowled at Moose Alley.

Earlier that morning, Buck had trotted out the door, failing to return by the time I'd secured the Grumman to the trailer, but with Father Brendan depending on my timely arrival at the boat ramp, I could not wait for the old dog to appear and had set a bowl of food on the floor of the screened porch before driving off. That's why I was driving west on Route 16 rather than lying in bed beside Bailey.

Turning off the blacktop, I could hear the sound of the Grumman's aluminum hull clanging against the trailer as the truck bounced over the rutted surface of the Morton Cutoff Road. About to turn left onto the Lincoln Pond logging road, I slowed for a large pickup that turned in front of me. The American-made truck had lights above the cab and a brush guard protecting the grill.

Although there was no moon, I could tell by the light of the stars that it was a black Silverado coming down off the flank of the Cupsuptic River, the same road we had taken the previous week to fish the pond above the stream. I hadn't had the opportunity to ask Arthur, Jr. about his father and how he came to be driving such an expensive truck. There weren't any camps that far up the river, and I never knew Arthur, Sr. to show any interest in fishing. Curiouser and curiouser.

Still mulling over this puzzle, I turned onto the Green Top logging road. Maybe he stole the rig, but then wouldn't it have been reported missing? And Arthur was certainly making no attempt to hide his use of the vehicle. Stopping at the Camp Ten Bridge, I concluded that he had to be running errands for one of the film crew. I looked down onto the Big Magalloway, where the previous afternoon Magalini had nearly drowned battling the trout of a lifetime. The light from countless suns had traveled through the distant past to set the river aflame as if with flecks of silver. When Doctor Who's police box failed to materialize, I pushed down on the accelerator.

By the time I pulled the Toyota beside my cabin, concern for Hollyhock Leventhal overtook my curiosity about Arthur Wentworth. It was after one o'clock in the morning, but I had hoped to find the lights on with Holly inside sipping a cup of tea. The stars remained bright as I trudged up the porch stairs. After piling the rod case and my duffel in one corner, I walked over to the green table, where I keep a battery-operated lantern. While searching for the button, I heard twittering and then a swishing sound. A moment later the prick of tiny claws dug into my shoulder.

Hazy light bathed the interior of the screened porch when I pushed in the button on the side of the lamp. Buck raised his head from where he lay curled on the floor and squinted in my direction as I lowered myself into a rocker. The bowl beside the rocker was empty.

"What have you been up to?" I asked, but the old dog had already lowered his head, his eyelids flickering and then closing. The flying squirrel that clung to my shoulder crawled down my chest and into my lap. The rodent that Buck and I had rescued as an infant scurried onto the table when he heard me turn the lid on the jar of cracked corn.

Closing my own eyes, I told myself not to worry about Hollyhock, that Ronnie would sort it out. My muscles slowly relaxed as I listened to Rocky crunching kernels of corn between his tiny teeth. When I opened them again, the sun was streaking across the landscape. Stretching my arms above my head, I tried to work out a knot that had developed between my shoulders. My face hurt more than my elbow, but the scratches on my hands were beginning to heal. Rising slowly, I bent forward and tried unsuccessfully to touch the toes of my boots. With my left leg still asleep, I balanced on my right, crossing over the dog, who remained motionless.

A flock of warblers swept into a nearby spruce. As I listened to their chatter, a woodpecker hammered in the distance. While I slept, spiders had spun their webs in the bushes outside the porch and the dew that had collected along the strands of silk sparkled in the sunlight. The pond rippled under a slight breeze, the last remnants of an early-morning fog slipping over its surface. I grabbed the binoculars and glassed the water, stopping to watch the circles of a trout's rise until a large doe on the far shore caught my attention. As I adjusted the lens, the big deer came into focus. Her white tail erect, ears folded forward at attention, she stood just beyond the tree line. Hesitating for a moment, the deer strutted down to the water. I was wondering whether she was the doe that had given birth when her two fawns came trotting out of the shadows on their little legs. Had it only been a week and a half since Holly and I had watched them come into the world?

Beside me, Buck had opened his eyes, and then with a loud groan, flopped back on his side like a large chub thrown onto the bank. After a moment he righted himself, stretching first his front legs and then his back. On all fours, the black Lab lumbered toward the screen door, and after nosing it open, trotted down the steps and out onto the wet grass, where he squatted for a few seconds before turning down the path that leads to the pond.

I looked around the porch, checking behind my duffel and then between the garden tools that leaned in the other corner. Climbing up on a stool, I found the flying squirrel curled in a mouse nest built of twigs and spruce needles hidden in the shadows on top of a rafter. The rodent blinked twice before climbing into my open palm, purring as I carried him inside the cabin and up the stairs to my bedroom. After taking a long drink from a bowl of water, the little guy crawled onto the shelf in my closet and into the long wooden birdhouse that sits on its side. While I pulled a pair of shorts and a clean tee from a drawer, Rocky began shredding a few tissues and by the time I'd stripped out of my clothes the squirrel had dragged the shredded pieces behind him, using them to close off the little hole he had entered.

I grabbed my bathrobe from a chair and limped back down the stairs in my fleece-lined moccasins. While pulling a towel from the rack behind the bathroom door I caught a glimpse of my face in the mirror. I looked like I'd gone the distance with Mike Tyson.

Outside, chickadees and titmice twittered on either side of the narrow path as I tramped down to the pond, the little birds flitting among the branches of the spruce and balsam. I wondered what would happen when Ronnie Adams met up with Horace Baker. Like bends in a river, so many questions.

Trout continued to dimple the pond's surface as they fed on spinners left over from the night before. The sun that rose above the mountain ridge had fallen behind a passing puff of cloud. Except for a single shaft of light that illuminated a small section of the far shore, all fell under shadow. While waiting for the sun to reappear, I stripped the bandage off my elbow and checked to be sure the scrape had not become infected.

This past winter Bailey had urged me to see a physical therapist for my hip and back, which I did, driving down to Farmington each week, but stopping once I moved back into my cabin. As the sun slipped back out from behind the cloud, I went through the exercises the therapist had prescribed and quickly worked up a sweat.

I had nearly completed a series of stretches when a female merganser floated past the large, flat boulder beside the pond. Her brood followed, eleven by my count, swimming in single file, one or another lowering its head under the surface while they quivered and quacked. I wondered how many would survive through summer. Like the two fawns, they would need to beat the odds to make it through their first season. I wished them well, telling myself that for now, at least, the living was easy, as the little column swam behind their mother, the springtime sun warm against their feathers. Turning to hang my towel on a nearby popple, I found that Buck had materialized out of the forest.

I swam out three hundred yards or so, and raising my face, treaded water while the sun bathed the wound on my cheek. After a few minutes I turned back. Buck, who had watched from beside the boulder, waited until I was within fifty yards of the shoreline before swimming out to greet me. The pain in my elbow returned with each stroke, my lungs burning, as the dog, whistling through his nose, swam beside me.

After drying off, I climbed atop the boulder while Buck wandered along the side of the pond, sniffing at this and that before once again disappearing around a bend in the shoreline. I tried to recall the last time we two had swum to the other side of the pond.

Some men seek power, prestige and wealth, but I found neither fame nor fortune provided solace when my world fell off its axis. Others look to religion in their time of need, but after my wife died, leaving me with an infant daughter, I left California, finding meaning here, beside these tannin-stained waters rather than under a roof enclosed by bricks and mortar.

With my eyes closed and legs crossed, my mind began to slowly clear while I chanted a phrase that my old friend, the poet Gary Snyder, gave to me. My aches and pains began to fade as thoughts of Buck's youth, Bailey and Danni Donovan, Hollyhock and Horace Baker, black trucks, poachers and the Millers all receded while the mantra that sounded a lot like *spaghetti and meatballs* floated out over the surface of the pond.

I'm not sure how much time passed. It could have been a few moments or maybe an hour when something began scratching at the boulder beside me. Opening my good eye, I looked down to find a Canada Jay, its head cocked to one side. Ignoring the gray bird that was about the size of a robin, I once again closed my eye, but thoughts of the past and present conspired against me.

After moving back east from California, I spent my time learning the water, trails and logging roads that spread out through the dense forest where moose graze and black bear make their dens. Along the way, I nodded to lupines, trilliums, and Joe Pye weed, the beaver and mink, loons and mergansers, but until meeting Bailey had no one with whom to share my stories.

I was old enough to know that Danni Donovan wasn't about to slow down long enough to listen to my tales, but was Bailey's recent indifference a sign that she too had lost interest in them? And why was I drawn to the reporter when we had so little in common? And where the hell was that dog anyway?

A second jay squawked from the King's tree on the other side of the path while a third answered from somewhere farther back in the forest. Judging from the size of the bird beside me, it had only recently fledged from the nest, the two parents calling from the safety of the trees while the youngster, yet to learn fear, waited for a handout.

Some say Canada Jays, or Whiskey Jacks as they are also known in western Maine, received their name from the hard-drinking loggers of times gone by, but Richard Morrell claims that the name is a modified form of a Native American word for trickster. I reached inside a pocket of my robe, but found nothing. Trying the other, I pulled out a few bits of Rocky's corn. Without hesitation, the Jack hopped closer. After plucking the kernels from my open palm, the brash bird flew into the trees and then followed its parents down the shoreline.

Abandoning my attempt at meditation, I concocted the beginnings of a yarn involving the young trickster, two fawns and eleven baby mergansers. If the adults in my life had lost interest in my stories, I could always count on the Lafleur kids for a rapt audience.

Chapter Eighteen

When Buck didn't return from his walk, I climbed down from the boulder and trudged back to the cabin. After changing the bandage on my elbow and dabbing some ointment on my cheek, I slid on a pair of overalls and ate a breakfast of oatmeal sprinkled with cinnamon and sliced banana. Back on the porch, I grabbed a bucket from among the shovels, hoes and other long-handled tools that leaned against the far corner, found my work gloves and limped down the steps and outside, where the sun still shone. I had been working the water nearly nonstop since the ice went out, and was happy to have a few hours to myself.

A rambling affair, my vegetable garden is always in flux, sometimes contracting, other times expanding, depending upon the extent to which I fall prey to the siren's song. Like gardeners everywhere, I'm addicted to the winter catalogues with their colorful pages of bright flowers and succulent vegetables, and like most anglers, I can't wait to open my L.L. Bean catalogue advertising all of the latest fishing gear.

Tramping over to last season's garden, I swung aside the chicken-wire door and surveyed the remnants of the previous year's crops. Withered vines and leaves hung haphazardly from metal cages and wooden trellises, the well-worked soil pitted and heaved after the long Northwoods winter. By August, the garden beds would extend outward from the mulched paths, providing a jungle of produce, but as May came to a close there were few crops to till.

The snow peas I planted earlier in the month had broken through the soil, their green tendrils reaching for the first rung of the chicken wire. Beside them, potatoes remained protected from the cold nights under the long mounds I'd dug for them. In one corner of the garden, I inspected radish seeds that had germinated, and in another, the tiny leaves of recently planted spinach, lettuce and arugula. I filled the bucket with leaves and other debris that had collected around the remnants of Italian parsley and oregano, and after clearing the little patch of herbs, turned to the chives that had also weathered the winter.

Bailey too enjoyed gardening, planting flowers in front of the bookstore and in the yard behind it. Thinking back, I realized she hadn't been out to the cabin since last fall. While cleaning the beds of winter detritus, it dawned on me that the chores I once enjoyed now seemed dull without a partner to share them.

My hip clicked when I walked around the wire fence that stretched between cedar posts to keep out deer and other animals. Checking for holes around the bottom, I searched for signs that rabbits, woodchucks or porcupines had burrowed underneath. I'd dug the wire a foot under the earth for just this reason, but over time it had a tendency to rust and break, residents of the nearby forest ready to breach my fortifications at the first sign of weakness.

Maybe it was the difference in our ages or the fact that Sam Treadwell appeared ready to swoop in should he get the chance, but I worried that Bailey had lost interest in not only my stories but also the storyteller. I tried to remember a time when she wasn't a part of my life and how it might be if that changed.

I repaired one section of fencing where the old wire appeared brittle and shored up a post that had heaved. Earlier in the spring Finley MacDougall had dropped off a pile of sheep dung in exchange for a couple dozen flies, patterns to match the flying ants that periodically hatch throughout the fishing season. Satisfied that all was secure, I spent the remainder of the morning raking the manure into the garden beds. Once done, I stuffed my work gloves into the back pocket of my overalls and walked over to the cabin. Back from his travels, Buck sat by the steps, where he stared in my direction.

After fixing the dog a late breakfast, I poured a glass of white wine. Poking my head into the refrigerator, I came out with a crock that held the remains of a chicken marsala dinner. I freshened up the sauce with a few of Richard Morrell's mushrooms, poured in some additional wine and heated the contents on the stove. Breaking off a chunk of fresh French bread, I dipped it in the bubbling gravy.

Buck followed me outside after we ate our meals. Sniffing around the wild blueberry bushes, the old dog ambled over to a flowerbed where he barely raised a hind leg. I remembered that first year Bailey spent time with me. How she carried burlap bags full of lupines and foxgloves from the back of her Jeep and how we spent the remainder of that afternoon planting the little bed of perennial flowers. I wished she were with me now.

Walking over to the lean-to on the far side of the vegetable garden, I pulled out the smaller of my two chainsaws. Earlier in the spring, I'd had Junior sharpen its teeth and tune the engine. After checking to see that it was filled with both gas and oil, I walked to the edge of the forest to work on an oak that had been uprooted during a winter storm. I hadn't heard Ronnie Adams' Explorer come down the drive, the sound of the chainsaw reverberating in my ears as the young warden waited for me to take a break before calling my name.

While I set the saw on a stump to cool, Ronnie lowered a knee to scratch under Buck's neck.

"You don't look much better than last night," he said when I walked over.

"I don't feel it," I replied.

"Fair amount of wood." The warden reached out a hand to shake mine.

I had cut up the tree's mantle, retaining the wider limbs to burn in my stove and dragging the smaller branches into a brush pile. There was a line of sawdust wherever the saw had cut through the oak's trunk, a pile of fourteen-inch logs stacked to one side.

"It's a beginning." I pulled off my cap and used it to swat away a few black flies.

"Might get a mess of downed trees if that storm they're predicting swings our way." He looked around at the forest that surrounded the small clearing.

I pulled out a neckerchief from the pocket of my overalls and wiped the sweat from my face while trying to ignore the familiar cramp in my lower back.

"Can't recall a hurricane making it this far north so early in the year," I replied, repeating what the guy on the weather station had said.

"Think we could check out the spot where you saw my friend?" Ronnie appeared preoccupied.

"Give me a moment to wash up," I said, lifting the chainsaw off the stump and carrying it toward the lean-to.

Ten minutes later we were driving along the two-track between my cabin and Hollyhock Leventhal's camp while I described what I'd found up on the Little Magalloway. The warden, who was calling in our location to his dispatcher in Augusta, held up a hand when I began to tell him about the deer Jeff Lafleur had discovered.

"Already been down to see him," he said, clicking off the receiver.

"You think it was Baker?" I asked.

"Hard to say, but if it was, he was too smart to leave any evidence behind."

"Not all that smart." Horace Baker had been poaching for as long as anyone could remember without receiving a fine, until the county magistrate handed down the two-year jail sentence based upon the young warden's intensive investigation and subsequent testimony at trial.

Ronnie kept his eyes on the two-track as he spoke.

The warden pulled his Explorer off to the side when I told him to stop. A few feet away we could hear Otter Brook flowing through the metal culvert.

"This is where Holly parks her van." I looked down at a set of ruts in the soft earth of the abandoned logging depot. "From here she hikes up to her camp." I pointed to a narrow opening in the otherwise dense forest.

"And you're sure this is where you saw Baker?" Ronnie called from the other side of the culvert.

"That's where he was parked." I walked the short distance to another pair of ruts on the opposite side of the road.

The warden turned toward the back of his vehicle. Inside, he opened a daypack and pulled out two pairs of latex gloves.

"Put these on." Ronnie handed me a set. "But don't touch anything," he barked.

Usually deferential, the warden had spent the last few weeks chasing a phantom and his frustration was beginning to show. He retraced his steps, but slower this time, until he came to the ruts made by the paleontologist's van.

"Stay put," Ronnie called over his shoulder.

Ignoring the warden's command, I followed him into the forest, where he entered the wood through the narrow opening used by Hollyhock to walk up to her camp.

Grunting his displeasure, the younger man pushed aside spruce branches and ducked under those of poplar and birch. He followed the narrow footpath for a minute or two before stopping.

"There," he called. Ronnie examined a print in the mud, tracing the outline through the thin glove.

"Pointed tip. Elevated heel. A man's boot like the kind Bobby wears, but larger."

I pictured the Tony Lamas preferred by Bobby Mendez, the border patrol agent, who had been born and raised in Texas.

"Another. Also a man, but smaller than the first. Looks like a work boot," the warden called a few moments later. "And another. This one more like a sneaker."

"I don't like this. Holly's camp is only a few hundred yards from here." I leaned against a tree while the warden took his bearings.

"Look, for all we know Baker was taking a piss by the side of the road when you came upon him."

"What about the prints?" I asked.

Ronnie started up again without answering.

After a few minutes more I could hear the brook falling down out of the dilapidated wooden dam at the southern end of Otter Pond. A moment later we walked out of the forest and into a clearing. Hollyhock's campsite consisted of two large box-like canvas tents with a table and chairs set between them. A tarp was stretched from one tent to the other to protect the furniture from the elements. It looked peaceful enough, except that the paleontologist was nowhere to be found. I called out her name while walking up to the dam.

After following the brook downstream, I returned to find Ronnie opening the flap of one of the tents. I slipped in after him and sat on the cot where Holly slept when not at my cabin.

"Same as when I found it," I mumbled.

"Get off," the warden growled.

I wasn't used to being told what to do and glared back at him.

"This could be a crime scene." He stared back at me until I rose.

"But you said..."

Ronnie had already turned away. He scanned the top of a folding table that contained a number of small bones and a few arrowheads as well as other unidentifiable bits of forest bric-a-brac. Removing a pen from his breast pocket, the warden flipped open the clasp on a footlocker packed with books. I identified a few fly-fishing how-tos among the paleontologist's scientific journals. Next, he zipped open a large suitcase that contained Holly's neatly folded clothes.

"Wherever she is, she didn't take her fishing gear." I pointed to a rod tube that leaned in one corner of the tent. Her waders and vest hung in another corner, where I'd seen them the previous morning.

We found a cooking stove and sink in the second tent. A few yards away, the paleontologist had rigged a second tarp to form a lean-to for a gasoline generator used to pump water from the brook.

"Not including yours, I count a few more prints heading in both directions. The larger ones similar to the boot prints we found along the trail, the smaller print the same as the one that looked like a sneaker." The warden looked through the cooking utensils arranged on a wooden cabinet that also contained an assortment of canned goods.

I reminded him that Holly wore Converse sneakers.

Along the edge of the forest, we found a plastic toilet under a third tarp stretched between two trees. I followed Ronnie as he circled the tents, but neither of us could find anything out of the ordinary. Although I had been to the campsite as many times as Holly had been to my cabin, I couldn't find any sign that something might be amiss.

But where would she have gone for such an extended period of time? Did she travel back to the Midwest without telling me? Ronnie said he'd check the Rangeley airport to see if Holly had flown out of there.

The warden pulled a pen and pad from his breast pocket. Scribbling a note, he tore out a page, thought for a second, and then walked back inside the paleontologist's sleeping quarters, coming back outside with a roll of duct tape. Ripping off a piece, he taped the note to the table under the tarp.

"I told her to check in at your cabin after she comes back."

"You mean *if* she comes back."

The warden saw the expression on my face and shrugged his shoulders.

"After checking out her camp, I'm more concerned about the poaching, but in either case I intend on looking up our Mr. Baker, I promise you that."

Ronnie slipped the pad back into his breast pocket.

Unable to think of anything else to say, I followed him into the forest. We retraced our steps past one of the paleontologist's dig sites, turning around at the old dam and then working our way downstream, each of us covering a different side of the brook, until we came to the culvert. On our way, we inspected two more of the paleontologist's excavations for foul play, but found nothing except a few more prints.

"No signs of a struggle. Nothing you'd call suspicious." The warden pulled off his cap and scratched his head. "Looks pretty normal to me."

"They could have surprised her coming in from the forest."

"I suppose, but why?" The warden returned his cap to his head. "Look, Horace is close in height and weight to you, and that boot print is at least a size twelve. Besides, he's a loner. I've never known him to have a partner."

Back on the road, Ronnie once again studied the scene. He walked up one side of the two-track and down the other. A few feet above the ruts made by Baker's truck, the warden placed a cigarette butt into a plastic zip-top bag he pulled from a pocket along his thigh.

"What now?" I asked as we tramped back to his vehicle.

"Now I pay Mr. Baker a visit while you go about your business."

Chapter Nineteen

On the short drive back to the cabin Ronnie assured me that Holly's sudden disappearance was, in all likelihood, not connected to Horace Baker. The warden promised to keep me in the loop, but when a sport canceled an outing for the morning before my dinner date with Danni Donovan, I decided to pay Mr. Baker a visit. I had been to his cabin only once before. It was a few years back when I bartered a few dozen flies and a basketful of vegetables from my garden to reduce the price on what is now the larger of my two chainsaws, the one that still starts on the first pull of the cord.

The weather had remained fair until the night before last, when a warm front brought clouds from the south. Although it had been raining since I woke, it was what Hollyhock liked to call a soft day, with little evidence of the monster storm the forecasters continued to predict for our region.

I stretched forward to look into the Toyota's rearview mirror. Blood swelled around a black-fly bite on my neck, but the swelling on my cheek had gone down. I had been bouncing over the logging road that runs down the east side of Green Top Mountain, Buck curled beside me on the passenger seat. Turning left at a fork in the road, I scratched at the bite while turning again, this time a right, when the road forked a second time. With each turn, the two-track narrowed. I'd hoped to remember how to get to Baker's camp, but suddenly found myself on a dirt road that appeared abandoned. Rainwater filled in the ruts on either side of a median where tall grass bowed with moisture. The rain-laden branches of alders scratched the sides of the truck as I downshifted into second gear. From a disc in the CD player, Warren Zevon asked for lawyers, guns and money, which, I thought, might come in handy about then.

I pulled the Toyota into a small opening by the side of the road. Leaving Buck in the truck, I slipped up the hood of my poncho and walked out into the rain.

Horace Baker was not a man who appreciated surprises, so I figured it best to simply walk up to his cabin and hope he'd give me a chance to explain my presence before taking a shot at my head. Turning up a bend in the road, I hesitated, feeling the hair on the back of my neck go up as the cabin came into sight. Whenever entering a berry patch, it's always wise to make some noise so as not to startle the black bear that may be snacking on one of its favorite foods, but with the rain coming down harder there was little more to be done, except to dodge puddles while hoping the man inside did not have me in his sights.

The camp's buildings were similar to most, a one-story cabin and a few outbuildings, one to store wood, another equipment, and a third for Baker's generator. The cabin was dark, and like the other structures, it appeared as exhausted as the dead and dying equipment strewn around it.

When not breaking the law, the poacher repaired and then sold what others had abandoned for junk, hauling it out of the Rangeley dump. With rain dripping off the bill of my cap, I scanned the yard in front of me. Lawn mowers in various states of disrepair shared the grounds with a broken-down snow machine and an old Ford 8N with a rusted bucket loader. Alongside the aged tractor stood a number of refrigerators, a three-legged woodstove and two lawn tractors, one up on blocks and another with its engine removed. Nearby, a white porcelain bathtub collected water beside a sink with weeds growing out of it.

Farther back, along the edge of the forest, the skeletal remains of a DeSoto lay among the frames of at least two trucks dating back to Prohibition as well as what I guessed to be a late-model Cadillac.

"Looking for somebody?"

I swung around as a figure materialized from the shadows along the far side of the cabin, a state-issued sidearm in his hand.

"Jeez-a-wee," I cried out.

The warden, who had an uncanny ability to appear out of the forest when least expected, wore camouflaged rain gear.

"You gonna tell me what you're doing here?" Ronnie Adams frowned. Although holstering his weapon, he stared toward the cabin, glancing from side to side while waiting for my explanation.

"Last I heard it's still a free country."

"And you thought you'd just wander in here and get your head blown off," the warden cut me off. "I suppose you parked your truck up around the bend?" he grumbled.

"You suppose right," I answered.

"You hear from Holly?" the younger man asked.

"Not a word," I replied, waving off a small squadron of black flies.

"I guess we should get out of this rain." Ronnie turned toward the forest, the cloud of bugs following him into the shadows.

I nearly bumped into the warden when he stopped a few yards beyond the tree line.

"Buck back at your cabin?" he asked.

"Sleeping in the truck."

Ronnie zipped open a small tent that I had not seen. Its camo coloring made it nearly invisible against the rain-soaked forest.

"Home away from home," he muttered.

Lifting the flap, Ronnie followed me inside. The warden handed me a mug he pulled from a backpack and unscrewed the cap from a thermos. The dark liquid that poured out looked more like sludge than coffee. Ronnie explained that he hadn't found anything to link the poacher with the deer or the fish I'd found on the Little Magalloway.

"I double-checked both sites, but there's no way of tracing either back to Baker or anyone else." The young warden sat cross-legged inside the tent.

The coffee tasted worse than it looked.

"There hasn't been anyone around here since I set up shop last night. You saw the road. It hasn't been traveled in quite some time. It looks pretty much the same as it did when I dropped by in early spring, although the shutters are now off and the cabin well stocked with provisions. Whoever's been coming and going has been doin' it on foot."

"You got anything to eat?" I asked, hoping to remove the taste of the coffee.

Ronnie pulled an energy bar from his backpack and tossed it to me. "I was waiting to see if Baker might show up when I heard your truck bouncing down the road." The warden looked tired, his eyes red, stubble across his face.

"You find out anything about Holly?" I asked.

"The airport has no record of her leaving. I asked Jeff if he had seen her. He said she dropped in to buy a couple bottles of wine. According to him it was late on the same day you last saw her."

I stared back at the warden.

"Look, before leaving my trailer yesterday, I called the university. A professor there said she rarely checks in while out in the field."

It had been nearly three weeks since the paleontologist had spent the night at my cabin. I swallowed a chunk of energy bar. It tasted as bad as the coffee. Outside, the rain had slowed.

"I think we should give Holly a few more days before calling in the cavalry." Ronnie opened the flap and flung the remainder of his coffee out into the rain.

I was still frowning when he looked back at me.

"I don't like this any more than you do, but she could have taken off with friends. Maybe she's exploring another site."

I still didn't buy it and told the warden so.

"I'm gonna hang here." Ronnie trudged back toward the forest. Over his shoulder, he called, "I'll be back in town by noon tomorrow. If you don't hear from me before then, I'll leave a message with Christine." With that, the younger man vanished back into the shadows.

Chapter Twenty

When I returned to my cabin Hollyhock Leventhal was not waiting with a cup of tea. I checked to see if she had left a note with one of her smiley faces drawn on it, but could not find one. The rain continued throughout the afternoon. After starting a fire in the woodstove, I peeled off my wet clothes and stepped into the shower, turning the water up as hot as my old bones could withstand.

I knew that the notorious poacher wouldn't think twice about protecting his illicit activities, even if it meant hurting a woman. Horace Baker had a reputation for being a mean son of a bitch, one who didn't give a damn about the law.

After staying in the shower for some time, I slipped into my flannel bathrobe and fleece moccasins and shuffled into the kitchen. Grabbing a Sam Adams from the fridge, I heated up a bowl of minestrone soup and carried it to the easy chair beside the woodstove. Buck, who had curled up on his cushion, looked at me, his nose twitching at the scent of food.

I had nearly forgotten about the Millers' financial worries. Magalini had paid for his two days on the water, adding a hefty bonus, enough to bring their payments current with plenty left over for my needs, including the purchase of that little rod in the window of Sun Valley Sports. I was looking forward to giving them the good news.

Ronnie's note could have been blown away in the storm and Hollyhock might not be aware that we were concerned for her safety. I thought about changing back into my rain gear and hiking over to her dig, but the following day would be a long one. The next morning I was scheduled to guide three sports staying at Beaver Den Camps, and later that evening to meet Danni Donovan for dinner. Ronnie had Baker's scent. I'd have to rely upon the warden, at least for now.

While lying in bed, I formulated my game plan for the next day. After spending Friday afternoon guiding sports, I'd stop by the Millers and then shower and change my clothes at Bailey's. Although I had stopped at the bookstore one afternoon earlier in the week and slept over at Bailey's apartment the following night, she continued to be preoccupied, shrugging off any suggestion that something was wrong. We had said little, and I still hadn't told her about Danni Donovan's dinner invitation.

I pulled the wool blanket up around my chin. While slipping in and out of sleep, I decided to ask Bailey to drive down to Bethel with me. We'd spend a weekend at the Inn there, and after purchasing the cane rod, enjoy a Sunday brunch before returning home. I might even convince the Millers to come along, the four of us staying in one of the Inn's fancy suites now that they'd be flush again.

The next morning, the rain had stopped, the sky once more blue. After a quick breakfast of tea and toast slathered with butter and Beldora MacDougall's blueberry jam, I walked out onto the porch. Buck was lying in the sun and did not look interested in spending another day on the water. Replenishing the dog's bowl with food, I rustled his fur before collecting my gear.

Tom Rider's head guide was booked to spend the morning trolling on the lake and the owner of Beaver Den Camps had recruited my services when his other guide dropped an outboard engine on his foot. I pulled in front of Tom's fishing lodge a little after nine, rustling up the three men, all in their fifties, two of whom lived in Indiana, the other in Massachusetts. College buddies, they had remained friends over the years, each season fishing in a different locale. After transferring my gear to their SUV, I slid into the passenger seat and directed the New Englander up the logging road along the west side of Aziscohos Lake. After driving over the small bridge that traverses the Little Magalloway River, we passed by Long Pond, a few minutes later stopping at the road that leads to Parmachenee Lake.

After unlocking the gate, I directed the driver toward an indentation along the southern end of the lake known as Black Cat Cove. There are few cabins in the Parmachenee tract and no utilities, but because of the ongoing logging operations, the roads were well maintained by the paper company, allowing us to move at a swift clip while the three men bantered about politics. The two Midwesterners sitting in the backseat espoused the virtues of less government while the guy behind the wheel turned now and again to chastise his buddies about the broken economy left by the former president.

"If Obama had his way, the Feds would ban fishing so the tree huggers could have the streams to themselves." The guy seated behind me turned to his friend, who nodded approvingly.

As we swung down off a height of land, I made out Richard Morrell's camp. Sheltered among stands of spruce and white birch, the Wabanaki had built his cabin upon a grassy knoll overlooking the east shore of the lake, where he could watch the sun set over the hills that marked the northern New Hampshire border.

"But you need clean water for trout streams, and if you guys had your way, big business would be able to pollute our air and water." Looking for support, the driver turned toward me.

"Spoken like a true comrade of the People's Republic of Massachusetts," growled one of the sports in the backseat.

When the man beside him asked where I stood on the issue, I knew better than to give my opinion. Remembering how a small number of individuals nearly destroyed the pristine beauty of Otter Brook, I bit my tongue, explaining that politics and trout fishing did not mix. This didn't seem to slow them down, the conversation turning heated as I instructed the driver to park above the remains of an old wooden dam that at one time raised the water level of the Magalloway River to allow logs to sweep freely over the tops of boulders that these days protrude above its surface.

After they collected their gear, I led them into the forest. The conversation that had turned to evolution came to a halt as the three men waved their hands through a cloud of black flies, members of a species that to my dismay had come out on top according to Darwin's theory. Hoping smoke would ward off the bugs, one of them lit a cigar, but the biting did not slow down until we waded into the lake, the black flies never as bad on the water as along the bank.

After crossing above the beams of the dam, we waded single file up the far shore of the cove, where I set each man far enough apart to avoid any further debate. Starting them off with streamers, I switched to wet flies as the morning progressed and dry flies when the fish began to look toward the surface.

I spent the following two hours tramping up and down between the three sports, answering their questions, pointing out likely lies, and changing patterns while hoping they would lose themselves in the sights and sounds of the Parmachenee wilderness. Throughout the morning, I shared my bug dope with them, a concoction that Richard Morrell had come up with using the region's natural plants and resins, the three men slathering it on their faces, necks, wrists and hands.

Sometime after eleven the Wabanaki appeared from between the spruce and balsam. Wearing a high-top Stetson with a turkey feather sticking out from the band, he sauntered over to my side. The Vietnam vet had braided his black hair into a long ponytail that hung down between his shoulders.

"Was thinking of taking them over to Little Boy," I said as Morrell approached.

"Been fishing well. Moved a brook trout and three salmon the day before yesterday."

"Any size?"

"The brook was a hog, three, maybe four pounds. The salmon were okay, fifteen, sixteen inches each."

I started walking toward the nearest sport, motioning for him to pack it in.

"Big weather heading our way." The black flies appeared to ignore the Native American.

"So I hear," I said.

While we talked about the tropical storm and whether it would continue along its path toward New England, I pulled out the bottle of dope and rubbed a few more drops into the neckerchief I wore around my neck.

"What's in this stuff?" I asked.

"Old Indian trick." He chose not to elaborate further.

We spoke for a bit longer, after which the Wabanaki faded back into the forest as quietly as he'd appeared.

No sooner had I collected my sports than they resumed their argument, moving from Darwin's theory to prayer in the schools and from there to taxes and the deficit, continuing the debate while we drove around the western edge of Parmachenee and up along the little ponds above Indian Cove. I figured they'd stop when we parked, but as we hiked down the narrow trail that leads to Little Boy Falls, the two Midwesterners continued to mock the New Englander's views, telling him that like the president, he was a socialist.

They quieted down only when we came into sight of the river, the three of them hurrying toward the pool below the falls where a few years earlier I was pressed into duty, guiding the Vice President of the United States. Bolted to a boulder beside the picturesque site is a plaque donated by the Maine Federation of Republican Women commemorating the afternoon President Eisenhower cast his flies in the same pool.

The three sports walked over to a picnic table set a short distance from the plaque. While they checked their gear, I unpacked our lunch, eggplant smothered in my own tomato sauce and placed between slices of thick French bread. By the time they finished, the sky had turned overcast, and I suggested that they switch to Blue-Winged Olives.

Although one of the Midwesterners tied on a nymph, the other insisted on casting the streamer he had been using earlier in the morning. I left the first man below the falls while walking the other a short distance downstream to the wide, smooth run called Landing Pool. Promising to return shortly, I directed the third sport back up the narrow trail, hiking past his vehicle and across the logging road. After climbing down a steep trail, we stopped at another wide run known as Cleveland Eddy.

"This is where I bring the Democrats to fish," I told the New Englander.

After tying a Blue-Winged-Olive imitation with a parachute wing to his tippet, I handed my sport another, as well as two emerger patterns, telling him to switch if the dry flies didn't produce.

As the afternoon progressed, I once again moved from one sport to the other. A little before four, I left the two men and humped back up the logging road to pick up the third. Back at their vehicle, the three friends compared notes. While packing away their gear, I listened to the conservative-minded anglers describe the five fish caught between them, the New Englander releasing fourteen trout, two that measured sixteen inches or more and a large salmon that broke him off.

On the ride back to the lodge one of the guys from Indiana wondered out loud why his friend from Massachusetts had caught so many fish. I wanted to explain that ever since the Republican Congress attempted to gut the Clean Water Act, the fish of western Maine tended to vote Progressive. Instead, I turned and repeated an old saw known to most anglers.

"That's why they call it fishin' instead of catchin'," I drawled in my best Dud Dean imitation.

Chapter Twenty-one

"I thought a thank-you was in order." Danni Donovan leaned forward and poured the final drops from an expensive bottle of Chardonnay into my glass.

An hour earlier, Ricky Wilkinson, the same young man who had taken an interest in Donovan at the bowling alley, had rolled a cart into her hotel room, setting out a pheasant dinner on the oval table where we now sat back and savored the wine.

"This wasn't necessary," I replied, swirling the bright golden liquid against the sides of the glass.

I rose and drew back the drapes from a window that took up most of one wall. Staring out at Rangeley Lake, I looked up at a sliver of moon, the first few stars beginning to appear.

"But I owe you, Sal. You have no idea what a coup this is for me."

I turned to Donovan, who had pushed back her chair and walked to my side, her hand circling my waist.

I had left the sports at Tom Rider's lodge a few minutes after five and didn't make it into town until six. Rather than stop at the Millers to discuss my plan to help them bring their loan current, I drove straight to Bailey's apartment. After showering, I had changed my clothes while describing the reporter's ambush outside the bookstore and how afterward, during lunch at Kim's, I had arranged for her to interview the maestro in exchange for rearranging my schedule to accommodate his desire to spend time on the water.

"I was glad to help," I mumbled to the reporter, taking another sip from my wineglass while continuing to stare out onto the moonlit lake. Donovan's hand moved from around my waist to the small of my back, her breath now against my neck.

Bailey had been lying on the couch, her feet up, wrapped in a blanket. She wasn't sure whether arranging an interview with the film's director would distract the reporter from airing a story about me, but was happy to hear of my intention to use Magalini's generous fee to bail the Millers out of their financial jam, saying that the sooner they brought their mortgage current, the better the chances Rusty might find his way back from the bottom of the bottle.

Donovan raised her hand toward my cheek.

"Looks worse than it feels," I lied. The bands of color below my eye had gone from a greenish-blue to a dull gray. As the gash began to heal, the swelling receded, but the right side of my face hurt whenever I bent down.

I had explained to Bailey that the dinner was a mere courtesy, something I couldn't refuse. I expected her to complain, but she didn't. Perhaps it was because of the way she had been acting over the last few weeks, or maybe it was my attraction to Danni Donovan that was becoming hard to deny, but I found myself eager to leave the apartment. Walking into the Northwoods Inn, I was surprised to learn that dinner would be served in the reporter's suite rather than the hotel's mahogany-paneled dining room.

Donovan now faced me. Behind her, the lake shimmered in the moonlight. "So what do you say?" she asked.

The reporter chuckled when I took a step back. Turning, her heels evaporated into the plush rug as she crossed to a large dresser facing the queen-size bed that dominated the spacious room. Donovan slid open the doors that concealed an entertainment unit. Shifting toward a desk beside the dresser, the woman looked up into a gold-trimmed mirror. After rearranging a few disobedient strands of hair, she set her wineglass down and pulled a disc from her purse.

I stared up at a large oil painting enclosed in an ornate frame that hung on the wall across from the bed. In the foreground a few ducks lazed among some reeds while farther back a set of hills rose gently to touch a pale blue sky. I was thinking how nice it would be if life could be that peaceful when the theme from *Hollywood Tonight* filled the room.

"Ready?" Danni Donovan had slipped the disc into the DVD player below the television and was patting the bed beside her.

The show's hosts reminded me of life-size dolls, their teeth nearly as dazzling as those of Father Brendan while they announced the interview with Bruno Magalini.

Fast-forwarding through a commercial, Donovan reiterated how the director had fulfilled his end of the bargain, granting her an hour of his time. She explained that the interview had been cut down to fifteen minutes, which would air in three-minute segments over five consecutive nights during the following week. I could feel her body next to mine and was finding it hard to concentrate on her words.

Breaking the spell, I walked back to the table. Donovan followed, grabbing her empty glass from the desk and sitting across from me. She thanked me again and motioned toward the cart. I uncorked the second bottle of wine and replenished the reporter's glass while Ken and Barbie filled the screen with their perfect features, the two talking heads bantering about the making of the movie, until the camera faded to a large body of water, which I immediately recognized was Hawley Pond.

Donovan leaned forward, clinking her glass against mine. As the camera panned away from the sunlit water, I glimpsed a familiar vehicle parked among the tents and trailers along the shoreline. Beside the black Silverado were two men engaged in conversation. I recognized Arthur Wentworth, Sr., a cigarette dangling from the corner of his mouth, but the camera moved too quickly for me to get a look at the other man.

My mind shifted away from Arthur and the Silverado when the Great Magalini came into focus. The maestro's golden hair fell down around his shoulders, his one eye flashing with intensity while the brim of his black fedora drooped down over the patch that covered his other eye. Seated across from him, Danni wore a navy blue jacket over a white blouse that revealed her sleek throat and a hint of what lay below. A skirt that matched the color of the jacket rose up her shapely hips. She had worn her hair up for the interview.

As the famous director used the reporter's questions to paint a self-serving portrait, my mind once more slipped back to Arthur Wentworth and why he might be at the set of my daughter's movie. Like Junior and Merle Lansing, was he looking to make some easy money as an extra?

The camera remained fixed on Magalini's face, never moving below his chest, while on more than one occasion it swept from the reporter's face down her neckline and over her legs, leaving the viewer with the illusion that interviewer and interviewee were of equivalent height.

When the first segment ended, Danni hit the button on the remote, fast-forwarding until the second interview began. Sometime during the five short pieces, my attention turned toward the attractive woman seated across the table from me. This evening, her hair fell down over the shoulders of a cocoa-colored blouse that betrayed the outline of her bra. She had left the two top buttons of the blouse open. Brown heels complemented a tan skirt that was not as short as the one she'd worn during the interviews.

"Now if I can just get the elusive Mr. D'Amico to agree to speak on the record." Donovan raised her glass, a Mona Lisa smile slipping across her lips.

"How 'bout you settle for my daughter and leave me out of the equation?" I asked, my eyes held by hers.

"How 'bout we forget about interviews and just relax for the rest of the night?" The reporter lowered her glass and walked back to the bed, where she used the remote to click off the television. Leaning forward, Danni Donovan slipped off her heels, massaging a foot through a stocking that matched the color of her blouse.

"It's really not fair. I'm stuck in pantyhose while you look much too comfortable." The newswoman padded past the open window and over to the table.

Sliding onto my lap, she raised her arms around my neck. Brushing her lips against my cheek, she lowered them to my mouth. For a moment I found myself responding, but then drew back. The reporter cocked her head to one side. Her expression reminded me of a confused dog, albeit a very attractive and desirable purebred.

"It's nothing, Sal, just a few hours of fun, my way of saying thanks."

I grabbed the wine bottle and bending forward, returned it to the cart. Donovan, still seated in my lap, unlocked her hands.

"That's the point, Danni. Maybe if it was something, but like you said, it's nothing, and what I have with Bailey, well, that's real, and I don't want to be the one to screw it up."

"Why, Salvatore D'Amico, I think you might be the last gentleman on the planet." The reporter leaned over and bit me on the ear. "You know, I don't usually take no for an answer. Hell, I'm not sure if you deserve a slap or another kiss."

"I have that effect on people," I said, rubbing my ear.

Standing, she grabbed her glass and took a long sip of wine.

"Friends?" While her eyes held out the promise of more, she extended her arm in my direction.

We both laughed as I cautiously reached out my hand to shake hers.

A few moments later Donovan excused herself. When she closed the bathroom door, I poured myself a glass of wine, drinking it down in a series of quick gulps while standing at the window, looking out onto the lake. Off to one side, in the shadows cast by the thin slice of moon, I caught movement, maybe a deer coming up from the shoreline or perhaps a moose. I let the thought go.

When the reporter returned, she was wearing a cream-colored cashmere sweater and a pair of designer jeans. I noticed that her feet were now bare.

By the time Ricky Wilkinson knocked on the door, we had finished the second bottle of Chardonnay. I moved out of his way as the young man pulled the cart from beside my chair, lips curled into a pretentious smirk. While he transferred the remains of our dinner, Donovan stared down at the menu. Looking up, she whispered, "Since I can't have you, how about we share some key lime pie?"

What the hell, I thought.

Chapter Twenty-two

"It's not like we're married." Bailey had her back to me while arranging and then rearranging the same three books on a shelf beside the door of her store. "I mean, you can see whomever you like," she continued, brushing by me as she began adjusting another set of books along a shelf on the opposite wall.

When I'd first entered, Bailey had acted even more distant than of late. Only after I asked if there was a problem did she let loose with both barrels. Apparently, Danni Donovan had sold another story, this one picked up by the gossip papers and then by the cable stations. Even one of the networks had run a piece, including a photograph of the two of us in the reporter's hotel room.

I followed Bailey into the small office in the back of the store, where she sifted through some boxes.

"I thought you were all about flying under the radar?" She bustled past, still not making eye contact, books piled high in her arms.

After saying goodnight to Donovan, I had driven back to my cabin, spending the next couple of days guiding sports, while returning to my camp each night. Taken completely by surprise, I was finding it hard to believe that the reporter had betrayed my confidence, especially after I had arranged her interview with Bruno Magalini and promised another with my daughter. Perhaps I didn't know her as well as I thought.

Although I had taken three ibuprofen, my aches and pains ached and pained me more than usual. Crossing between the two dogs, I lowered myself into one of the easy chairs and stretched out in front of the Jøtul stove that remained as cold as Bailey's countenance. Rose's tail thumped the floor as I reached down to scratch the top of her head. *Good old Rose*, I thought.

"But that's the only reason we met," I pleaded my defense. "She was thanking me for the story on Magalini. I agreed to give her access to Pru and she promised to keep me out of it."

Bailey set the books out on the round table beside the magazine rack, the table where my novel had been displayed the last time I'd been in the store.

"And I suppose you had to seal your little deal with a kiss?" She grabbed a gossip rag and tossed it at me. On the cover was a photograph of Donovan seated on my lap, her hands locked around my neck, our lips coming together. The line under the photo read, *"Famous author Salvatore D'Amico, aka Stephen Rocco, finds love on the set of the movie based on his daughter's books."*

"Really, Sal? I thought we had something." She stared down at me, tears welling up in her eyes.

I was at a loss to explain the photograph, unable to understand how it had been taken. It was just the two of us in the room, and although I couldn't imagine her being that desperate for a story, it was hard to come to any conclusion other than the fact that Donovan had deliberately shanghaied me.

I called to Buck, Rose whining as we walked through the door. Bailey said nothing. Outside, the sun peeked out from between the clouds. Leaving my truck parked in the gravel lot beside the bookstore, I trudged the short distance up the street to Lakeview Sports. Upon our arrival, Buck collapsed on the wooden decking of the Millers' porch. I left the dog adjusting his frame on the planks that had been warmed by the sun and entered the store.

Jeanne stood behind the counter while two men wearing fishing vests bent forward, the three of them listening to the weather forecast on the radio. She looked up and frowned upon seeing it was me. In a rack beside the door, the headline on the front page of the *Boston Globe* declared: **TROPICAL STORM ANGIE GAINING INTENSITY**. Walking over to the counter where the Millers sell their flies, I opened the cover of the plastic display case and bent over to check out the patterns inside.

"What the hell?" I screamed a few moments later.

As soon as her customers were out the door, Jeanne had walked over and slammed a closed fist into my biceps.

"How could you?" She landed another punch, harder than the first.

"Jeez-a-wee," I groaned, massaging the upper part of my arm. "It's not like it seems."

"It seems pretty bad," she countered, as I stepped back out of her reach. "You want some tea while you tell me your sad story?" she asked.

I waited until she unclenched her knuckles before replying. "I'll take a root beer."

We sat on stools behind the register while I explained about my dinner with Danni Donovan. I stopped once when a family came in looking to rent a canoe for the afternoon, but continued after Jeanne resumed her seat.

"I set up an interview for Donovan with Bruno Magalini. The dinner was her way of saying thank you. It was all perfectly innocent. I agreed to set up a meeting with my daughter and Donovan agreed to leave my name out of her story."

Jeanne grabbed a newspaper from under the counter and opened it to the photograph of Donovan seated on my lap. "That ain't my idea of innocent." She raised the bottle of pop to her lips and drained the remainder of its contents. "You do know this photo has gone viral?"

I scrunched up my face in confusion.

"The Internet, you big dummy." Jeanne shook her head from side to side.

"It was just the two of us in that room and I didn't see any cameras," I pleaded my innocence.

"Men," she hissed.

Wanting to speak with both Millers at the same time, I now decided against it. Hoping to improve my standing with Jeanne, I pulled an envelope from the pocket of my jeans and pushed it across the counter.

"Look, I didn't do anything wrong. In fact, I'd like to think that I did something right," I said.

"What's this?"

"Part of my deal with Magalini. Way more than the usual fee for two days on the water. He paid enough to bring you guys current with plenty left over for me."

"We can't take this." She pushed the envelope back in my direction.

"You can and you will. Consider it a loan if you want." I rose from my stool.

Jeanne wiped away a tear with the sleeve of her denim work shirt. Standing up, she threw her arms around my neck and while on the toes of her leather work boots, kissed my cheek.

"Women," I whispered.

That's when she connected with her third punch.

"So where's your old man, anyway?" I asked while trying to ignore the pain in my arm.

"After driving to the bank to ask for another extension, he was heading over to the Nickel to have lunch with some of the boys."

"You're a little low on wet flies." I pointed to the display case.

Jeanne looked down at the envelope. "We'll take three dozen and two more of your nymphs."

Standing on the porch, I took a deep breath. The black flies had emerged, but here in town they weren't bad. Even with the plague of biting insects, the warmth of June was welcome after the long winter and cold, damp spring. I looked down at the dog, but he didn't stir. I wished that we could have changed places. A few feet away the Hawley River bounced along on its current, unconcerned about the affairs of mankind.

Buck opened his eyes when I nudged him with my boot. Reluctantly rising to his feet, the old dog hobbled down the steps. His legs, at first unsteady, took a few moments to adjust while we walked down the main street of town.

Sam Treadwell sat on the bench outside his office, his face sheltered by the brim of the Boston Red Sox cap that he had pulled down over his eyes. A few weeds sprouted from the flower boxes hanging under his office window. As I turned toward the Wooden Nickel, the veterinarian called to me. Stopping in the parking lot outside the roadhouse, I waited while he unfurled his frame and ambled across the main street of town.

"Screwed up big-time, huh?" It was hard to tell if his smile was meant to convey sympathy or sarcasm.

Tired of explaining myself, I shrugged my shoulders. The veterinarian followed me inside, where we took seats at the counter alongside Rusty and Richard Morrell.

"What'll it be, fellas?" Betty Leonard walked out from the kitchen, her heels tapping against the pinewood floor. She wore black pants that hugged her slim figure. Her breasts pushed against a not-quite-satin blouse the color of an apple on an October morning. Snapping a stick of gum, the waitress blew a big bubble, popping it back into her mouth while taking Sam's order. When I finished giving her mine, she rolled her eyes, saying, "Would you like a side of reporter with that?"

There were times when I hated living in a small town. The cramp in my hip hadn't stopped aching all morning and the pain below my eye competed with that in my back, making me feel my age.

"How 'bout a couple of aspirin instead?" I asked.

"Guess you beat me out for number-one screw-up," Rusty muttered, staring down at his coffee mug through bloodshot eyes.

I arched my spine, testing the limited strength in my lower back.

"You're in the shit, my friend," muttered Morrell, who forked a mess of scrambled egg from his plate.

I frowned in his direction.

"Just sayin', " he added.

"What did the bank say?" I asked the guide.

Rusty explained that the loan officer had been out to lunch.

"No matter," I said. While his eyes remained fixed on the counter, I told the guide how Magalini had paid me enough to bring his loan current.

Betty returned, pouring a Coke into a glass for Sam and placing a bottle of root beer in front of me. Removing a bottle of aspirin from her apron, she popped off the lid and handed me two tablets.

Pushing the bottle toward Rusty, she muttered that we both looked like crap.

I chased the pills down with a long pull of the root beer while the guide waved her away.

"Suit yourself." Betty grabbed the bottle before turning back to the kitchen.

"Can't wait to see the look on that punk's face." The guide raised his mug to his lips and swallowed hard.

Betty returned after a few minutes carrying Sam's hamburger and fries on one plate and my grilled tomato-and-cheese sandwich on another. I picked up one half of the sandwich and took a bite, letting the flavor fill my mouth. There's something to be said for comfort food.

"I don't know how to thank you, Sal." Rusty turned, looking me in the eye for the first time in weeks.

"You don't have to say anything. Just go home and give Jeanne a hug, and then wash up, and for Christ's sake, put a cork in that damn bottle."

Richard looked up from his eggs and mumbled, "Whatever you do, don't let him kiss you."

Chapter Twenty-three

Back outside, Buck was feigning interest in a teenage girl while her boyfriend looked on with a bored expression. When the girl bent forward to extend a hand toward the old dog's chin, I grabbed the candy bar held in her other hand and gave it to the boy.

"You may want to hold this out of harm's way." I stared down at the Lab, who glared back up at me.

The sun had retreated behind a bank of clouds, a few drops of rain falling on our shoulders. Sam trotted across the street and into the shelter of his veterinary while Rusty and I turned up the block, increasing our pace, trying to make it back to his place before the heavens opened up. Reluctantly, Buck followed, the old dog turning back to stare at what he determined was rightfully his.

It began to drizzle by the time we came into sight of the sporting goods store. Jeanne had come out onto the porch, and it took a moment for me to realize that the tears running down her cheeks were not those of joy. Sensing his wife's distress, Rusty took the steps two at a time, Jeanne nearly collapsing into his arms. It took another few moments for the usually stoic woman to gain enough composure to tell us that soon after I had walked down to the Nickel, the bank officer had called to say there would be no more extensions. With her voice trembling, Jeanne told us that he had declined to accept her offer to bring the loan current, stating that the time to do so had expired.

"He said the case is now in the hands of their lawyers and the only thing that can prevent foreclosure is payment in full."

"That's over two hundred and seventy-five thousand dollars," Rusty muttered as he held his wife tightly to his chest.

"There's gotta be some mistake," I said.

"I told him we would bring the money down today, but he just kept saying it was too late and that it was out of his hands."

Jeanne was inconsolable. Rusty walked her inside the store and up the stairs to their apartment while I sat behind the counter. Buck remained curled on the braided rug beside the door when an hour or so later the guide stomped back down the stairs.

"I'll take it from here," he said, explaining that Jeanne had cried herself to sleep.

"She's gotta have it wrong. No way they can do that," I assured him.

Rusty lowered his head into his hands.

He didn't answer when I told him that no matter what happened, he had to quit drinking. "Jeanne needs you now more than ever," I pleaded.

I hung around the store for another hour, my platitudes sounding hollow. The rain had stopped but the sky remained overcast. Walking back to the bookstore, I decided it best not to go inside. Instead, I helped Buck into my truck and drove out of town.

There was no way the Millers could raise such a large amount of cash, and I felt responsible. Making their pain worse by raising their hopes, my guilt was compounded by the fact that I could have dropped off the money before the May deadline had expired if not for my dinner with Danni Donovan. While driving over the stone bridge at the entrance of town, I came to the conclusion that the reporter had lured me to her room to gain publicity with photographs taken by a camera she had hidden somewhere in the suite. Our relationship, as short as it was, proved one thing—predicting the behavior of fish is far easier than that of people, especially those of the female persuasion.

I turned east at Koos Knyfd's bear and drove past Grasshopper Hill, where a farmer had mowed the field while leaving grass to grow in the form of the letters *U S A*. Ten minutes later, I pulled into the town of Rangeley, passing Moose Alley and stopping beside the Builders Supply Store to allow an SUV with New Jersey plates to turn into its lot and park between two other out-of-state vehicles.

Business in town was picking up. Tourists wearing sandals and shorts walked the sidewalks. There was a car parked outside the fly-fishing shop while families sat around tables under the awning outside the Red Onion restaurant.

Driving past the Morton & Furbish Real Estate Agency, I stopped again, this time to allow an elderly couple to shuffle across the street. I didn't want to believe that Donovan had set me up, but could think of no other explanation. The question was why. After I had arranged an interview of a lifetime and promised one with my daughter, why did she feel compelled to use me for some free publicity? The only way to find out was to ask her.

I pulled to a stop outside the Northwoods Inn. Cracking the windows in the cab, I left Buck snoring on the passenger seat. The sun slid out from behind the clouds, illuminating the rows of pansies planted on either side of the stone walkway that led up to the stately hotel. Drops of rain from the earlier shower sparkled like diamonds on the flowers' purple, yellow and blue petals. I ignored the click in my hip while climbing the granite steps and opened the Inn's massive oak door.

I stood for a moment, wiping the bottom of my boots on a mat before walking inside and crossing over an Oriental rug with lush maroon and green tones. On the other side of a mahogany counter, the college-age receptionist wore her blond hair in a bun and a simple pearl necklace over a white blouse that she had buttoned to her neck.

With her hand over one end of the phone, the young woman whispered that she would be with me in a moment. While she continued her conversation, I surveyed the large room. Above the mantel of a massive stone hearth hung a painting of a waterfall that descended through a mountain ravine. In the foreground stood a bull moose with a regal-looking rack. Staring out from a plateau, the animal appeared to be surveying his domain.

There were paintings on the other walls, each glamorizing a different outdoor scene. One had a covey of partridge milling around a spruce tree and in another, three black bear cubs peeked around their mother, a large sow with mournful eyes. Herb Welch had painted a third, this one of a leaping brook trout. A true Renaissance man, during the 1900s Welch had been a celebrated artist, taxidermist, guide and entrepreneur known throughout the region.

The head of an enormous trout protruded from a plaque on the wall behind the counter where the receptionist was finishing up her call. Enclosed in glass, the fish's cavernous jaws held every conceivable pattern of streamer and wet fly.

The way I heard the story is that around the turn of the nineteenth century reports came in from Upper Dam of a brook trout as smart as it was large. By 1923, Shang Wheeler, a sport of many seasons and friend of Wallace and Carrie Stevens, wrote an ode to the char that he called White Nose Pete.

By the nineteen forties, the fish had become better known as Pincushion Pete, and sometime during the war a photograph surfaced of Shang holding the head of a giant trout mounted under glass. According to Graydon Hilyard, who wrote the definitive book on Carrie Stevens and her contemporaries, nothing had been heard of Pete until 1995 when the mythic creature was sold at auction to an anonymous bidder. But like Pincushion, the location of the actual mount had remained a mystery until purchased by the owners of the hotel.

"Sorry about that, but with all this news about the storm, we've been getting a lot of cancellations." The young woman behind the counter brought me back to the here and now.

When I asked whether Ms. Donovan was in, she looked at her computer screen. After clicking a few keys, she told me that the reporter had checked out the previous morning.

Walking back outside, I found that a light drizzle had returned. The rain's intensity increased as I drove back past Koos' bear.

By the time I turned down the Morton Cutoff Road, Buck was sitting up in the passenger seat, staring out at the waterlogged branches that closed in along either edge of the dirt-and-grit thoroughfare. I rolled over a metal culvert, the lights of the faded orange truck cutting through the dank afternoon gloom, occasionally slowing for potholes whose depth could no longer be judged now that they had filled with water.

After sliding a disc into the aftermarket CD player, the sound of mandolins, fiddles and guitars filled the cab. David Bromberg's band worked overtime to convince me that I'd find my way back to Bailey. An hour later, I pulled beside the cabin and trudged toward the porch while Buck trotted down the path to the pond, a dog on a mission.

Rocky was chattering from the shelf in my bedroom closet, the tiny rodent climbing up my arm and riding on my shoulder as I hobbled back down the stairs to let him spend the remainder of the dark afternoon behind the safety of the porch's screens.

I took three more ibuprofen before stripping out of my damp clothes. Standing under the shower, I did not leave until the scalding hot water turned lukewarm.

Chapter Twenty-four

I allowed the morning to creep over my consciousness, my mind slowly clearing while remnants of dreams, dark and confusing, swept past like clouds before the storm. After a while, I reached up and gingerly touched the gash along my cheek. Opening my eyes, I stared up at the pine boards of the bedroom ceiling. I tested my elbow, flexing my arm a few times. Closing my eyes again, I stretched out a leg. After stretching the other, I arched my back while raising my arms over my head. Bringing my knees up to my chin, I repeated the movement a few more times before casting aside the sheet. Sitting up along the side of the bed, I looked down and found that Buck was not on his cushion. Scratching my head, I rose and shuffled across the room.

I grabbed my robe from the back of the chair by the oak desk where the flies I'd tied before going to bed were lined up in neat rows. Still groggy, I stared out the window and found that the previous evening's rain had abated, leaving behind a gentle-looking sky with a few cumulus clouds drifting lazily across a light blue canvas. Gathering the wet flies into a plastic container, I placed the nymphs in another and slipped the tiny boxes into the pocket of my robe.

Buck was once again nowhere to be found. After returning Rocky to his box on the shelf of my bedroom closet, I took another shower, waiting for the warm water to loosen my muscles.

Once dressed, I poured some pellets into the dog's bowl, and set it down on the porch where he'd find it. Sitting in one of the rockers, I pulled out the two boxes and spread the flies across the little green table while trying to avoid thinking about Bailey. I was looking them over in the sunlight, musing over the actions of the mysterious Danni Donovan, when I realized Horace Baker was standing on the other side of the porch's screen door.

"Didn't think you'd 'preciate me waitin' inside while you slept the mornin' away."

I slid the flies back into the plastic containers and shoved them into the pocket of my robe as Horace swung open the door. Walking past me, the lanky poacher sat in the rocker on the opposite side of the green table.

"Coffee?" I asked.

"Whatever you're havin' do me fine." He looked down at my mug of tea.

Baker sat back while stretching out his thin frame, his gray eyes staring out onto Otter Pond while I walked into the kitchen. He remained silent until I returned.

I was trying to find a way to ask about Hollyhock when he muttered, "See you still haven't found your lady friend?"

"No, we haven't." I stood, facing the man who was about my age. Whatever the guy's reputation, I wanted answers.

For a moment I saw a flame rise in those badger-like eyes, but it quickly faded as a crooked smile formed on his thin lips.

"No need gettin' your panties in a bunch," he grunted.

Drawing cigarettes from the breast pocket of his khaki shirt, Horace tapped the pack against the table.

"You and that warden hangin' 'round my cabin ain't gonna bring her back." After lighting up, he looked around for a place to toss the match. Before I could say anything, he rose and ambled across the porch.

"Don't know why he's been hanging around my camp when the problem is right under your noses." The poacher opened the screen door.

Flipping the match out onto the damp grass, he looked toward my truck and asked, "You got a gun?"

I frowned. I had nothing against hunting and bartered with others for venison and grouse, but never took up the sport.

Holding the door open, Horace Baker turned back in my direction. "Since I'm a felon I ain't allowed one. No matter. Why don't you get dressed and we'll fetch your lady friend." Horace Baker strolled out into the sunlight without another word.

With the sound of the screen door reverberating in my ears, I hesitated for a moment, wishing Ronnie would pull down my drive or Buck return from his wanderings. Worried for Holly's safety, and without any alternative, I slipped off my robe and walked back into the cabin.

A few minutes later, the two of us climbed the grassy lane that led to the two-track where he had parked his truck. We passed his vehicle and followed the road toward the culvert above the paleontologist's camp. The poacher said nothing as we approached the spot where he had been parked a few weeks back. Horace flipped his cigarette onto the ground and crushed it in the mud. I followed as he entered the wood across the road from where Ronnie and I had previously searched. Baker bushwacked through dense spruce and pine, after a few minutes stopping at what appeared to be a game trail.

"Half-mile or so and we're gonna come upon those that took your lady friend. You got to be quiet, keep your cool and follow my lead. Can ya do that, Mr. Fishing Guide?" His eyes flashed, and then without waiting for my reply, he headed up the trail. The poacher tramped along at a fast pace for perhaps ten minutes and then stopped for a second time, waiting for me to catch up.

"What the hell's going on here, Horace?" I asked while catching my breath. "I mean, you have me hiking up a deer trail in the opposite direction from Holly's camp."

Horace Baker removed his cap. He waved off a cloud of black flies before running his fingers through silver hair.

"While I was in prison, these frogs come down across the border."

"Frogs?"

"Hells Angels out of Montreal. They set up a pot farm. Big business these days. Cut a deal with a few of our locals to grow their product out of sight of the Mounties."

I must have been looking at him funny because he hesitated for a moment, but then continued.

"Anyways, I was keeping tabs on them, looking for a way to get my cut. That's what I was doing the night you come up the road."

"Jeez-a-wee," was all I could think to say.

"We reached a deal, me and the gang, them not trusting the guys from this side of the border to hold up their end. Amateurs, they called them, paying me to make sure they didn't screw up."

Staring at the felon, I wondered what I'd gotten myself into.

"Everything would have been fine and dandy and me making a few extra bucks, but then your lady friend had to stick her nose where it don't belong. Best I've been able to determine, she stumbled into their camp, and, well, they couldn't have her spilling the beans."

My concern for Hollyhock's safety must have shown, because Baker put up a hand. "Relax. The gang's not gonna hurt her, at least not until they get what they want. By now they've been in touch with the family. Asked for ransom. Problem is, once they get it, that's when they'll bury her."

A pot farm in the Northwoods. Hollyhock Leventhal held hostage. It all seemed surreal.

"Anyways, I don't cotton to hurtin' women. So here we are."

"Don't you think we should drive into town and get Ronnie or call the Sheriff's Department?" I didn't like the idea of the two of us taking on a bunch of drug dealers.

"Now where's the fun in that?" Baker chortled, the crooked smile reappearing. "Besides, I got me a plan."

With that, the poacher turned up the narrow trail. For the next twenty minutes, he worked his way through the conifers, but when the narrow path petered out, the wiry Baker turned toward me.

"It's this way," he mumbled.

While adjusting his direction, Horace scrambled around boulders and climbed over fallen trunks of trees. My shirt grew damp with perspiration, the black flies taking the opportunity to bloody my neck and arms. We continued for ten minutes more, ducking under spruce limbs and around balsam branches, stopping twice more for Baker to take his bearings. Each time, he checked a compass and then headed out at a brisk pace. I followed a number of steps behind until the poacher raised his hand.

"Careful." He pointed to his boot.

I looked hard before seeing a thin wire that was nearly invisible a foot above the forest floor.

"That's new," he whispered.

Baker lifted his leg, carefully crossing over the wire. Crouching low, he now moved at a slower pace, a few minutes later dropping to one knee. At first all I saw was more forest, but then my eyes adjusted and there, perhaps twenty yards in front of us, was a series of camouflaged nets that had been rigged over a clearing about the size of a football field. The nets had been tied to trees surrounding the perimeter and held up with poles dug into the earth.

"Weed's under those pots." Horace pointed to the long lines of plastic containers under the netting.

"Those are soak hoses," I whispered, pointing to the rubber tubes that curled like black snakes between the pots. "Been thinking about getting a few for my garden."

"Stay here," Baker whispered in a stern tone. Looking over his shoulder, he added, "If you hear gunfire, beat it back to the road and get your ass to town as quick as you can."

I watched the poacher circle around the clearing, quickly losing him in the dense growth of the forest. After a while, my hip and elbow began to ache. I was trying to ignore the black flies when a tap on my shoulder ran through my body like an electric current.

"It's like I thought. This time of day, there's only five of them, three working the crop while two stand guard." Baker had walked up from behind me and was wiping the sweat from his face with a dirty handkerchief.

"What about Holly?"

"Didn't see her, but I'm pretty sure she's inside that little shed on the far side of the field." He pointed across the clearing where a man sat on a bench, his back pressed against the wall of a tar-paper shack, the brim of a dirty Stetson low on his brow. An automatic weapon lay across his lap.

"So what's the plan?" I asked.

"Simple," he said while reaching a hand around to his back and sliding it under his shirt. When he brought his hand back out, Horace Baker was holding a revolver that he raised toward my face.

"Move," he growled.

First Donovan and now Baker. How could I be so stupid? As I stumbled into the clearing, a man came running from our left. He spoke in rapid-fire French that I didn't understand but that roused his partner, who leveled the assault weapon at my gut while moving in our direction. The guy with the automatic was twice my size, wearing a sleeveless vest over a dirty T-shirt. Looking down, I saw that he wore boots to match his hat, boots like those worn by Bobby Mendez. The man on our left had pulled out a Glock. He was tall, but not as large as the guy with the Stetson. He wore a bandanna tied around his forehead.

The three other men were clearly worker bees. Two of them tended the plants while the third shoveled compost into a wheelbarrow. They looked up for a moment, but then went back to what they were doing. I recognized the guy with the shovel. He was part of Joe Hawley's grounds crew, the one who'd whistled from the deck of Ollie Stubbs' store the afternoon Danni Donovan and I had lunch at Kim's Pizza Palace.

"*Bonjour, mes amis,*" called Horace, his lips once again forming a tight smile.

"*Bienvenue, Monsieur Baker,*" the man with the bandanna called back.

As he drew closer, the cowboy kept his weapon leveled at my stomach. "*Qui est votre ami?*"

"Found him sneaking around. *Il connaît la femme.*" Horace nodded toward the shack.

The guy with the assault rifle turned to the one with the Glock and said something in French that I didn't catch.

"What we suppose' to do wit' him, eh?" The cowboy scowled at the poacher.

"Hey, *mon ami*, I did my job. You do yours."

After conferring with each other, the two gunmen appeared to come to a decision, the one with the bandanna pushing the barrel of his pistol against the small of my back. He prodded me toward the edge of the field while his friend stomped back toward the bench in front of the shack.

When I turned my head around to look at Baker, the guy with the bandanna shoved me forward. "*Vite!*" he screamed.

That's when I heard a loud pop, and before I could turn around two more pops rang out. When I did turn, the man behind me was writhing on the ground. Blood pooled out from under him. His friend had toppled forward, overturning the bench and losing his hat, which now lay beside him. As the Canadian cowboy groaned, the poacher walked over and picked up the assault rifle.

"Don't just stand there looking pretty," Horace called. "Grab that gun before he decides to get up and use it." Baker pointed to the Glock that had fallen a foot or so from the gang member's outstretched hand.

Bile swirled up from my stomach when I bent down to pick up the revolver.

The three men from our side of the border had fled into the forest. I stumbled toward the poacher. After warning anyone inside the shed to stay away from the door, Horace Baker shot off the lock with a quick burst from the automatic weapon. My legs felt rubbery and I was having trouble focusing. I lost sight of Baker when he stepped inside, but a moment later, he walked back into the sunlight, Hollyhock Leventhal leaning against his side.

Chapter Twenty-five

I looked over at Horace, who had dragged the two gunmen into the middle of the field and was tying them back to back with rope he had found in the shed.

Holly sat on the bench that the poacher had propped up. Her hair, a wild tangle during the best of times, was matted and dirty. The clothes she'd slept in since her abduction were stained with sweat and grime. Her face was smudged with dirt. She looked tired, but otherwise unharmed.

"They going to be okay?" I stared down at the two men, their clothes soaked with blood.

"Do you care?" Baker checked his knots.

"Was all this really necessary?" I asked him.

"You do know that he was going to kill you?" Horace nudged the man with his boot. "Ain't that right, *mon ami*?"

"Maybe if you hadn't wrapped me up in such a nice ribbon, he wouldn't have felt the need," I replied.

"Better you didn't know." Baker stood beside Holly. To me, he added, "There weren't no other way." To her, he turned and asked, "You able to walk?"

"You bloody believe it," she answered, rising unsteadily to her feet.

Baker popped the hat back on the cowboy's head as we passed the two bound men.

"Feckers." Hollyhock looked down at them, the big guy grunting when she kicked him in the shin with her red sneaker.

The poacher wiped his fingerprints from the assault rifle. "Toss over that Glock," he commanded, wiping it with a cloth he had found in the shed.

"What next?" I asked. It was nearly an hour later, and Horace had climbed into his vehicle.

"You take care of missy here. Say whatever you want. Just keep my name out of it. Like I said before, I can't be seen messin' 'round with firearms. Far as you're concerned I was never here." He turned the key in the ignition and slipped his truck into gear. "Tell that warden of yours he can find me in the funny papers."

"Aren't you worried their friends might come after you?" I asked as he started to pull away.

Baker laughed. He hung his head out the window and said, "Let 'em try. The Angels may be hot shit up there in French town, but this here's my forest. Has been for some time now."

Holly wanted to go back to her camp, but I disagreed. Walking down to my cabin, I went inside and grabbed my keys while she waited in the truck. Buck came up the trail from the pond just as we were backing up, and I stopped to help him climb in between us.

According to the tale we'd invented, I accidentally stumbled upon the pot field, was taken prisoner by the two bikers, and tossed in the shed with Holly. Although we could hear the firefight we couldn't see outside, and when a stray bullet broke open the lock, we waited for some time before venturing outside. When we did, we found the two injured men tied together.

The bikers might contradict us, but I was fairly certain that with a big drug bust like this one, the authorities would accept our version of events.

"We'll be okay if we stick to the story," I assured Hollyhock, who stroked the dog's back while she stared out at the passing forest. When I opened my window to let the warm air sweep through the cab, she leaned back, her eyes closed for some time. When she opened them, the paleontologist let out a long, slow sigh. Scratching the top of Buck's head, she looked over at me and said, "Tha' were brutal, Sal."

"It's over, Holly, and you're safe now." I slowed the Toyota to a stop and waited for a logging truck to pass before pulling onto Route 16. On the tree beside the blacktop, the new sign that replaced the old sign for the Morton Cutoff Road had been removed.

I figured it was also over with Bailey. Tending to avoid drama, I prefer to pull back rather than engage. My only excuse, if anyone asks, is that I'm too old to change. While brooding over what an ass I can be, my mind drifted back to Danni Donovan. Although my interpersonal skills might be lacking, in the past I had been able to tell the good guys from the bad. Misjudging her baffled and angered me.

Since walking out on Bailey the previous afternoon, I had thought it prudent to stay away from the bookstore, let the water settle before wading back in to cast my fly, a strategy that works well when fishing. But pulling in behind Richard Morrell's truck, I couldn't think of a safer place for Holly to stay until things settled down.

When we entered the store, Bailey and Richard were huddled around a radio listening to a weatherman describe how the storm had been upgraded to a hurricane. Bailey raised a hand to her mouth when she saw Holly. As the two women embraced, the paleontologist began to sob for the first time since she had stumbled out of the shed.

It was a little before twelve. I had intended to drive into Rangeley and tell my story to the chief, but instead pulled into the parking lot in front of the Millers' store and stopped beside the police cruiser that was parked there. Inside, I found Jeanne Miller chatting with Whitney Parker. As I ran through the events of the morning, the left side of the young deputy's face grew taut while the right side, the side scarred by burns, remained motionless. I managed to leave out any mention of Horace Baker while sticking to my story.

"Don't leave town," Whit called over his shoulder as he raced out the door.

Jeanne and I followed the young man outside, stopping on the deck of the store as he sprinted to his car. We watched as the deputy spun out of the parking lot, the lights on the top of his vehicle a blur of blue and red, and listened to the siren as he drove over the stone bridge. We were still standing there when a few minutes later a second and then a third siren wailed in the distance, the remainder of Rangeley's police department heading west on Route 16.

"Rusty out guiding?" I asked Jeanne as we turned to go back inside.

"He's down at the Nickel," she replied, quickly adding, "having lunch with a couple of the boys."

"Ah, huh," I mumbled.

"Really, Sal. He hasn't had so much as a beer."

"He talk any more to the bank?"

"We tried going over the loan officer's head, even called the corporate offices, but no one seems interested in helping. Just yesterday, I drove over to Rangeley to talk with Dan Jenkins and he says that in the past most banks were willing to work with their customers rather than foreclose, but lately even the smaller ones are looking to cull out their dead wood."

I knew Dan, one of two lawyers practicing out of Rangeley. We had fished together a few times. Although I held lawyers in the same regard as snakes, ticks and river spiders, he seemed to know his stuff.

"He says the bank's within its rights. Once someone defaults, even for a few days, it can demand payment of the loan in full." She sounded resigned to her fate.

"Can't you refinance?"

"Dan says no bank is gonna provide financing to someone who has fallen behind in their payments, especially now, what with all the bad loans out there and the bigger banks in danger of going under."

"I don't know how you're holding it together." I admired this woman, who was tougher than most men I knew.

"What about you? Planning on patching things up with Christine?"

Instead of answering, I reached into my shirt pocket and pulled out the two tiny plastic containers. "I filled your order."

"She's hurt, Sal. She wants to hear that you love her."

Jeanne frowned at the puzzled expression on my face.

I bent over and kissed her on the cheek.

"What's that for?" she asked.

"For being you," is all I could think to say.

Back outside, I helped Buck out of the truck, the two of us walking the short distance to the brick building that serves as the region's post office. Inside, I sorted through a number of Kmart and Lowe's flyers, throwing them in the trash while rolling up a Cabela's catalogue and a few envelopes with my address handwritten on the outside and stuffing them into the back pocket of my jeans.

Crossing the street, I entered the Wooden Nickel while Buck once again waited beside the door. A decent crowd had gathered for the early lunch special. Looking around, there appeared to be a two-to-one mix of movie people and locals.

Magalini's chauffeur nodded as I walked toward the counter. He sat at a table by the door across from the Michael Douglas look-alike, who stared at me as I passed. Natalie Jennings strolled in their direction. She carried two mugs of beer in her hands. With her natural girl-next-door good looks, the actress did not require makeup.

"How you doing, Mr. D'Amico," she said while squeezing past me.

I turned to see LeBron rise from the table as Natalie sat down.

Gina Summers, the other woman who had been in Rusty's Rangeley boat the day Bruno Magalini dove into the lake, sat at a table with three men, her red hair falling down around her shoulders. The actress wore a sleeveless tank top that showed off her assets. A few tables away, Junior Ross held court among a number of men I didn't recognize.

I found Rusty seated with Bobby Mendez. They looked up from their meals as I walked closer. Bobby was wearing his uniform, a green shirt with the Border Patrol emblem over the breast pocket. Unlike his fellow agents, Bobby's green pants fell down over pointed-tipped boots, the kind favored by ranchers out West, and here in the East, by cowboy wannabes like the guy we had left bound to his fellow gang member.

"We on for next week?" he asked as I took a seat beside Rusty.

No wannabe, Bobby Mendez was built like a fireplug, a tough guy, Comanche on his father's side. In his early thirties, he had grown up in Texas, where he was posted upon graduating from the Border Patrol's training school, his first assignment working the line between his home state and Mexico. After two years, something happened out there in the desert, something he had not shared with me but that resulted in his transfer to the Rangeley station.

"Thursday. I'll met you at the turnoff beside Steep Bank Pool, but you had better bring your bug juice. The black flies are out in force." When Betty Leonard sashayed out of the kitchen, I ordered a cheeseburger and sweet potato fries.

I had been teaching Bobby how to fly fish when we discovered that the headwaters of the Cupsuptic River were being illegally dredged for gold. Since then, the two of us had gone out together two or three times each season.

The younger man did not wait for me to finish my story about Hollyhock's abduction. When he heard about the pot farm, he took a final gulp of his soda and bolted from his seat. The sound of his boot heels clicked against the hardwood floor as he strode through the crowded roadhouse.

"Was over to your place earlier and spoke to Jeanne," I said to Rusty, after finishing my story.

The guide set his sandwich down on the paper plate in front of him.

"It's not looking good." He pushed aside the plate with his half-eaten sandwich.

When Betty came back out of the kitchen with my cheeseburger and fries, she leaned forward. With her elbows on the counter and her chin resting on closed fists, she asked, "So how you boys doin' this fine afternoon?"

"I suppose we've seen better days." I squirted some ketchup on the fries before picking an especially crispy one out of the pile.

As Rusty slid a few crumpled bills across the counter, he grumbled, "That would about sum it up."

Betty blew a bubble with her gum, snapping it back between her teeth.

"You hear about the hurricane?" she asked.

Chapter Twenty-six

"Take a look at this!"

I had filled the Toyota's tank, and was replacing the nozzle when Junior Ross called to me. He was hunched over a portable television set inside the office adjacent to the two large bays where the young mechanic kept the town's vehicles running well past their prime. With Buck staring out the truck's back window, I walked under a newly printed sign that identified the station as WAYNE'S WORLD.

"They're saying Angie's picking up speed rather than slowing down, which is weird since most storms peter out once hitting land."

I counted out three tens, two ones and thirty-two cents. Setting my payment by the register, I leaned in to look at the map of the Eastern Seaboard that was spread across the television's screen. Different-colored lines swirled across the Atlantic like strings of spaghetti converging along the border of Connecticut and Massachusetts and swinging up toward northern New England.

It was a little after four on the same afternoon. I had followed the deputy's instruction to stay in town. After speaking with Rusty, I walked back to the bookstore to check on Hollyhock. While Bailey tended to the woman in her apartment above the store, I tried out my story on Richard Morrell, leaving out any mention of the poacher. Less than an hour later, another deputy showed up accompanied by two state police detectives, who insisted that a doctor examine Holly. After dropping us at the Rangeley police department, the deputy drove the paleontologist to Franklin Memorial, the nearest hospital which was located in Farmington.

Saying things didn't add up, the detectives went at me hard for over two hours. They continued until the chief called them out of the room. A few minutes later one of the detectives returned, telling me I could go, but that I should not leave the area. Back at the store, Holly explained that she too had stuck to our story when questioned by a third detective, who had been waiting for her at the hospital after the doctor pronounced her free of injury.

Although I had taken little interest in the tropical depression that had picked up steam after slamming into Cuba and then blowing through Haiti, people in town had been watching the storm's progress, concern mounting when it swept up the coastline of Florida and then Georgia, many lining up at Hawley's Landing to haul their boats out of the water. Now, standing beside Junior, listening to him ramble on about the storm's progress, I no longer could ignore the hurricane that was presently hurtling up the coast of New Jersey and due to blow through western Massachusetts sometime later in the evening.

"The computer models are predicting Angie will cut a wide swath through Vermont, eastern New Hampshire and western Maine before she dissipates over the mountains below Montreal." Junior looked up from the screen, where a guy from the Weather Channel stood on a dune somewhere along New Jersey's shoreline. The meteorologist pointed toward the waves that crashed down a few feet away as rain pelted him in the face. He had the hood of his rain-soaked slicker pulled tightly around a cap, his legs braced against the hurricane's winds.

Idiot, I thought.

The mechanic turned down the sound when the camera panned to an attractive woman who began a primer on hurricanes. She reminded me of Danni Donovan.

"When's it supposed to hit here?" I asked, as scenes of wild waves and broken-down buildings flashed behind the woman on the screen.

"The Weather Channel is saying tomorrow, sometime around noon, but look at this." Wayne pointed to a U.S. Geological Quadrangle map, one of many he had scattered over the counter. "I figure that she's gonna hit the White Mountains by nine, zip along their eastern edge and then swing down into the Magalloway Valley by around ten, maybe ten-thirty. She'll extend clear across the Kennebago Divide east to Saddleback Mountain." Junior traced a line he had drawn with a red pen.

"A lot depends on how she bounces off the Berkshires," he said. Staring back down at his maps, Wayne mused, "Could sweep down over the Connecticut River Valley and miss us entirely." Junior's finger followed another line, this one drawn in blue.

Listening to the mechanic's chatter was making me dizzy, until the sound of a horn caught our attention. Outside, an SUV with Massachusetts plates had pulled up in back of my truck. Two other cars stood on the far side of the pumps.

"Been like this all afternoon. Tourists getting out ahead of the storm." Abandoning his attempt to plot a possible third course for Angie, the amateur meteorologist trotted outside.

A quarter-moon visible in the late-afternoon sky made it hard to believe that an early-season hurricane was hurtling our way, although it did confirm that however wobbly the orbit of Wayne's World, the rest of the universe continued to chug along at its usual pace. I drove the short distance to the bookstore, entering for the third time that afternoon. Junior's former wife stood behind the counter.

"They're upstairs," Karen called as I approached the door.

Bailey walked out of her bedroom when she heard me enter the apartment. Closing the door behind her, she said, "Holly's having trouble sleeping after getting back from the hospital. I convinced her to take a long shower, and she's only now closed her eyes."

"That's good," I said, turning toward the television that was on, but with the sound turned down.

"We have to talk." Bailey walked to my side.

Unable to think of what to say, I pointed to the screen, where a network weatherman stood in front of a map with nasty-looking clouds swirling across the whole of the Mid-Atlantic states. Outside, Hawley Pond rippled in the sunlight.

"Hard to believe it's supposed to hit here tomorrow." Bailey stood beside me, staring out the sliding door of her apartment. Beside the pond, there was a great deal of activity around the film crew's tents.

"Guess you should prepare." I turned away from the glass door.

"I'll be fine. Rusty and Jeanne are coming over later to help board up the windows of the store."

"You have enough food and water for a few days?" I asked.

"All set. Walked over to Ollie's earlier, even bought some extra batteries."

"I'd better get back to camp and batten down the hatches there." I walked across the room.

"But—"

"The cops will have taken care of everything by now. I'll be back by morning. We'll have plenty of time to talk while we ride out the storm."

I didn't wait for an answer. After kissing her on the cheek, I walked back down to the store and collected Buck before driving back toward my cabin.

I had the feeling that Bailey wanted to discuss more than just Danni Donovan. Something was wrong, even before my photograph made it into the rags, and I wasn't looking forward to finding out what she had to say.

It was nearly dark by the time I pulled onto the two-track above my cabin. I was about to turn into the grassy lane that leads down to my camp when a county sheriff's deputy wearing his brown uniform and Smokey the Bear hat waved his hands above his head. What appeared to be a law enforcement convoy clogged the road behind him. Interspersed between state police and Franklin and Oxford County Sheriff's Department vehicles, I recognized the three Rangeley Police cars, Ronnie's Ford Explorer and two white SUVs with the green lettering of the Border Patrol printed across the doors.

It took a moment for me to realize that the young man striding toward my truck was the same officer victimized by Buck on the deck outside of Ollie Stubb's general store.

I rolled down my window and smiled, but the sheriff's deputy, his hand against an unbuttoned holster, asked me to step out of the truck. He had checked my license, registration and insurance card and was listening to me explain for the second time that I was headed toward my cabin when Ronnie Adams trotted up the road.

Staring at Buck, who remained in the truck, the deputy reluctantly gave back my identification after speaking with the warden. I waited while they huddled a few feet away. Ronnie motioned toward the lane that led down to my cabin, the deputy shaking his head as he turned and walked back toward the cars blocking the dirt road.

It occurred to me that the paleontologist's camp would be hit hard when the hurricane came through. After getting the warden's permission, I spent the remainder of the evening hauling Holly's stuff up to the cabin, doing my best to secure her tents and tarps before calling it a night.

Clouds had rolled in sometime after dark, the wind picking up throughout the night, but by the next morning, only a light rain tapped against the windows. Ranking weather forecasters right up there with lawyers, I still had my doubts as to whether we'd get any more than some wind and an inch or two of rain, which wouldn't be all that bad for the fishing.

With no television, satellite or Internet service, I turned on my battery-operated radio. Unable to obtain a clear signal from any of the stations transmitting from New Hampshire or Maine, I fiddled with the dial until hearing the CBC station out of Quebec.

While scrambling some eggs, I listened to a panel argue over whether an English-speaking food critic was biased against Francophone restaurants. After about ten minutes, a Canadian meteorologist with a French accent advised that the hurricane working its way through New England would run out of steam as it crossed the mountains separating the province from its southern neighbor. He cautioned the residents of Sherbrooke, the closest city on the northern side of the mountains above Aziscohos Lake, to prepare for strong winds and heavy rain, with lesser amounts of precipitation falling from Quebec City to the Magdalen Islands.

Earlier, I had climbed a ladder to nail a plywood board over the bedroom window, and after that nailed boards across the porch screens. Looking out the kitchen window, I shook some basil flakes onto the scramble of eggs while taking a bite of toast.

The wind now came in gusts that caused the tops of the balsam and spruce to periodically lash about while the leaves of the hardwoods flapped wildly.

After cleaning off my dish, I threw on a rain jacket and walked outside. The air had that pre-storm electric feel to it. I turned off the valve shutting down the propane that powers the stove, refrigerator and gaslights, and then slipped a wooden cradle around the tanks to shelter them from any fallen debris. There wasn't much to do to protect the garden except to pick as many vegetables as I could. Walking over to the lean-to, I removed the chainsaw bartered from Horace Baker. After adding oil and gas, I checked its twenty-inch blade, starting it up with only one pull on the cord. I did the same with my smaller saw that coughed into operation after three pulls. Shutting them down, I used bungee cords to hold both saws in the bed of the truck next to a wooden box containing a small tank of gas, a container of oil, my long-handled ax and a number of metal wedges. Walking over to the generator shed, I nailed shut the door.

Back inside the cabin, I checked on Rocky, making sure the flying squirrel had extra food and water set out on the shelf beside his box. The little rodent must have wondered what was happening, for he stuck his head through the tissues blocking the opening of the birdhouse, staring out bug-eyed from the darkness of his nest.

"I'll be back in a day or so," I told him before closing the closet door. By the time I locked the shutters on the kitchen windows, Buck had walked up from the pond and was sitting on the porch. I looked around and decided there was nothing more to do. Rain was now falling harder and the wind had also picked up. After sliding on a pair of waterproof pants, I stuffed the vegetables into a plastic bag, locked up, and for good measure pushed a large rock against the bottom of the porch door.

The authorities must have been more concerned with the hurricane than the pot field, because there was only a single county sheriff's vehicle parked farther down the two-track when I turned off my lane. A quarter mile down the logging road I stopped at a spring and filled a five-gallon tank with drinking water, securing the container beside the wooden box. I wiped the moisture from my face after sliding back into the cab and turned up the CD player to hear John Hiatt's gravelly voice over the sound of the rain. Buck settled in as we bounced along. At the junction of Green Top and the Lincoln Pond Road, I noticed a new sign, a rectangular board nailed to a large spruce, the words GET A COMPASS spraypainted across it. *Funny Bear*, I thought.

A group of teenagers staying at a wilderness campsite were carrying an ice chest out to their SUV. Parking beside them, I trotted over and helped break down their tents. After we collected the rest of their gear, they followed behind me in their vehicle, pulling up beside my truck when I stopped in front of a fallen tree.

It took only a few minutes to clear the road, but with the rain falling harder and the wind whipping the treetops above our heads, we were happy to climb back into our vehicles.

The teens followed when I turned down the Morton Cutoff Road. Not long afterward, a black Silverado appeared out of the rain. Driving much too fast for the conditions, the truck headed in the opposite direction. Between the swish of the Toyota's frayed wipers it was hard to make out the driver, although I had a pretty good idea who it might be.

Unable to resist my curiosity, I braked as the expensive rig vanished around a curve. Motioning for the teens to pass, I turned the Toyota back into the forest while they continued toward Route 16. After taking the right at the end of the Morton Cutoff Road, and making a quick left, I followed the Silverado's tracks that stood out in the rain-soaked grit. As with the other logging roads in the region, the mile markers had been removed, and when the American rig came to the next major intersection, it turned, but then came back down in reverse, continuing up the east side of the Cupsuptic River.

Since the only thing of any interest that far up the road was the river and above that, the pond, I wondered why either would draw the attention of a guy like Arthur Wentworth, who cared little for the lakes and streams where I found sanctuary. So what would he be doing headed into the forest in the middle of a hurricane?

As we continued, I followed the tracks over the first snowmobile bridge and then the second. The falls through the Canyon had picked up volume from the rain that was now falling in great waves against the Toyota's windshield. Behind me I heard a loud crack. Looking back I saw a massive spruce fall across the road. With both chainsaws in the Toyota's bed I had no worries about getting back, and accelerated, hoping the other truck had not gotten too far ahead of me.

I caught up with it a few hundred yards above the Canyon and waited just below a bend as the driver hesitated at the intersection of Wiggle Brook Road.

In the driving rain, without any signs to guide him, he appeared to be having trouble finding his way.

The wind continued to whip the tops of the trees, with leaves and small branches falling across the road. Between the gusts of wind and heavy downpour I was fairly confident that the occupant of the Silverado had not seen me. I waited a few minutes before creeping forward, then followed the tracks to the left, turning right a mile or so up the road, and pulling the Toyota to a stop on the far side of the little wooden bridge a few hundred yards below Cupsuptic Pond. Grabbing a flashlight from the glove compartment, I zipped up my rain jacket and slid the hood over my baseball cap.

"Stay here," I said to Buck, who stared at me as if to say he had no intention of going anywhere.

Once outside, I hesitated for a moment before turning toward the two-track where the rain-soaked alders formed a tunnel, their branches whipping back and forth in the wind. I remember pushing aside the small trees with the flashlight and hearing the sounds of the raindrops splattering against my shoulders. A moment later, a flash of light was followed by a brief moment of searing pain and after that darkness.

Chapter Twenty-seven

"Did you get it?" I heard someone say.

"Found it up that trail. Right where they said it would be," another man, his voice more familiar, answered.

"Let me see." The one guy handed something to the other.

I was having trouble focusing my eyes.

"I still think it's a dumb idea," the first man said.

I had been unconscious and was having trouble orienting myself.

"Look, they think we work for that idiot and not the other way around. When the product doesn't show up, it's him they'll come for and not us. Besides, his DNA is all over the truck. All we have to do is take care of your friend over there and they'll be coming at that dumbass from both sides of the border."

I heard the voices as if from down a long tunnel, my vision still blurry, my ears ringing. The sound of the wind, like a train rushing up the tracks, tore through the trees. A wave of nausea swept over me when I attempted to sit up. Nodding out again, I awoke sometime afterward. Although the rain had washed away much of the remnants of my breakfast, bits of scrambled egg remained lodged in my beard.

My throat burnt, the smell from the vomit filling my nostrils. I attempted to rise, but my legs, like rubber, collapsed. Staring at my reflection, it took a moment or two to realize that I was lying on my side, looking into one of the

Silverado's hubcaps. When I raised a hand to the back of my head, my fingers felt something sticky.

The wind rushed through the tops of the trees, the alders along the trail thrashing back and forth. I felt sick again and although trying not to, vomited for a second time. Pushing down the hood of my poncho, I let the rain splash against my upturned face, which made me feel better.

"Get up, asshole." A shoe slammed into my side.

"There's no call for that."

I was trying to place the voices, when a pair of large hands grabbed my shoulders and helped me to my feet.

"Sorry about this, dude." It was LeBron Hayes. Rain spilled down his face. He wore gloves like the ones Ronnie had given to me when we searched Hollyhock Leventhal's camp. A dark slicker fell to his boots. "Can you walk on your own?" he asked.

"I think so," I croaked. But when he let me go, my legs went all wobbly again, my knees buckling as I slumped back down into the mud beside the truck.

"Jesus, Hayes, just drag him." I still couldn't place the other voice.

The big man's hands circled under my arms, my heels sliding along the wet earth. I was still trying to focus, the other man no more than a blur.

"Arthur?" I heard myself croak.

"Prop him up against that tree."

I looked across at Sam Treadwell's canoe. Magalini's chauffeur had dragged me down the path to the pond.

LeBron Hayes taking orders from Arthur Wentworth? I had to be dreaming. Trying harder, I blinked once, and then again, and found myself staring up at Michael Douglas. *Some dream*, I thought. But why was the actor holding a handgun in my face?

A familiar sneer slipped across his lips. Not the actor, I thought, but his look-alike.

"LeBron, what the hell's going on?" I turned to the former fullback, who had taken a step back. His face glistened with moisture.

"Sorry, man, but you shouldn't have followed us." He shrugged his massive shoulders.

Still groggy, I asked, "Where's Art?"

"Who?" the Michael Douglas look-alike asked. He also wore gloves.

"Arthur Wentworth," I said.

"That moron's gonna take the fall while we walk away with the money." He held up a backpack, the sides bulging outward.

"You see, good-old-boy Art was just our go-between with the boys from Montreal." Douglas' twin laughed. It was a mean laugh. "These belong to your buddy, Arty." He pulled out another pair of gloves from the pocket of his trench coat. They were not latex, but rather the kind of gloves I used to work around my garden. He tossed them at me.

"If they fit, the jury must convict. Ain't that right, LeBron?" The would-be actor chuckled. It was a nasty chuckle.

"If the cops on this side of the border don't get him, the bikers on the other side will," faux-Michael jeered. "Meanwhile, we'll be back in L.A. spending our money."

I was trying to follow, but my head ached and my hip hurt. Feeling sick again, I tried to retch but only gagged.

While my head spun, LeBron's partner continued, "You see, we had this sweet deal going with the Hells Angels. They provided the muscle and money and we supplied the location and the product, but now that the cops showed up, the guys from Canada will be looking for someone to blame." He looked back at Hayes.

I'd seen enough whodunits to know it was never a good sign when the guy holding the gun confesses to his intended victim.

"I guess Art will have some splainin' to do," the look-alike concluded with his best Desi Arnaz impression.

A gust of wind howled through the tops of the trees. LeBron flinched when a large limb slammed to the ground a few feet from where he stood. The big man stared wild-eyed out over the water when another splashed into the pond.

"Enough," he growled. "If you're going to do this thing then get on with it and let's get the hell out of here." Magalini's chauffeur lumbered back up the path.

"Any last words?" Michael's shoes made a squishy sound when he took a step closer. They were the expensive kind, made in Italy, with tassels on the top.

It was my turn to chuckle and then laugh at the thought that the last thing I'd see before leaving this goofy world was those expensive, Italian-made shoes sinking into a big gushy moose paddy.

Mr. Square-jaw returned my laughter with a grin of his own until he looked down at his shoes.

"Fuck you," he spat.

Closing my eyes, I regretted not having the chance to say goodbye to Bailey. Otherwise, all things considered, I had enjoyed my time here on planet Earth.

"BEAR!"

I didn't notice any hitch in LeBron Hayes' stride as the former fullback weaved around a spruce, juking to the left over an exposed root, and then hurtling over a boulder as Magalini's driver sprinted past me into Cupsuptic Pond, where he took three, maybe four steps before sinking down to his knees. His accomplice spun around as a black bear rose up on its hind legs. Dropping the backpack, he shot twice into the animal's chest. The beast, thrown backward by the bullets' velocity, lay motionless across the trail. Another gust of wind blew through the trees.

"Help!" It was LeBron. Although no more than a few feet away, I could barely see him through the rain that stung my face. He had sunk to his waist, and the more the big man struggled, the faster the muck at the bottom of the pond sucked him down.

"I guess that leaves more for me." The faux Michael leaned the backpack against a tree and pointed the revolver at the other man. I shuddered when the sound of a single gunshot reverberated across the pond.

A thin trickle of blood descended from a tiny hole in the middle of LeBron Hayes' forehead. Having evaded his last tackle, the former fullback sank under the surface while his killer turned the pistol in my direction. Looking over his shoulder while he pressed down on the trigger, I watched the bear rise to its feet.

Just before the bullet slammed into my chest, I was thinking, *Boots, the damn thing is wearing black leather work boots.*

Chapter Twenty-eight

The light was blinding when I opened my eyes. Closing them for a moment, I blinked a few times while trying to adjust to the glare. I turned to find a woman standing a few feet away, her back toward me as she gazed out a window.

"Excuse me?" My voice was no more than a whisper.

The woman turned.

"Danni?" I croaked as she hurried toward me.

I must have lost consciousness because when I awoke, Bailey was sitting in a chair next to me, her head tilted to one side, her eyes closed. With some difficulty I lifted my arm and placed a hand on her shoulder. I felt pain across my chest and was surprised to hear myself moan.

"Salvatore." Bailey opened her eyes.

Over the next few minutes she explained how Richard Morrell had found me a few miles south of the snowmobile bridges on the Cupsuptic River road and how he drove through the storm to the hospital in Farmington, where the doctors had removed a bullet from my chest. Apparently, they were more concerned with the concussion I had sustained than the bullet wound.

"South of the bridges?" I could hear wind howling, but this time the sound came from inside my head.

A nurse walked into the room and checked my bandages. After fiddling with some tubes connected to my arm, she smiled, wrote something on my chart and walked back out of the room.

Keith Moon was playing a drum solo inside my head.

"Below the snowmobile bridges?" I repeated, my voice hoarse.

"That's what Richard said. What were you doing way up there in the storm?" she asked.

What was Morrell doing up the Cupsuptic and how did I get below the bridges? I decided it best not to say any more, at least until I had the chance to speak with him. Instead, I said, "How long have I been here?"

"Richard brought you in day before yesterday, late in the afternoon."

"What time is it now?"

"Ten o'clock," she said, "in the morning."

"Buck?"

"He's fine. Back at the apartment with Rose. Holly is keeping watch over them. She sends her best, by the way."

"And the store?"

"Karen's helping out. No real damage from the hurricane."

"And you?" I asked, afraid to hear the answer.

Bailey didn't reply. Instead, she stood up out of the chair and walked over to the window where sometime earlier I thought I'd seen Danni Donovan.

"Maybe this would be a good time to have that talk we've been avoiding." My voice sounded a bit stronger.

"Oh, Sal." Tears had welled up in Bailey's eyes when she turned from the window and walked toward my bed.

"Before you start." I was having trouble gathering my thoughts. "As far as Danni Donovan goes," I stammered, "I want you to know that—"

"Danni explained the whole thing," she interrupted with a smile.

"She what?"

"She's been to the hospital twice. Came as soon as she heard."

Bailey related how the reporter had come to the bookstore to find me. "She was in the store when Richard called to tell me what happened. Danni explained that she would have been happy to go to bed with you, but that you'd have nothing to do with it."

I was having trouble keeping my eyes open.

"She said I was a lucky woman to have someone so in love with me."

A doctor came in and picked up my chart from the hook on the wall. He looked young enough to be my son.

"How ya doing?" he asked.

"Fair to middlin', " I replied.

"Bullet nicked one of your ribs, but otherwise didn't hit anything vital. Through and through, like the police are fond of saying. Lucky you have such a hard head. We were worried about internal swelling, but I think you're out of the woods. Another twenty-four hours and we'll know for sure." He replaced the chart on the wall. Removing a penlight from the pocket of his white jacket, he flashed it back and forth between my eyes. I repressed the urge to vomit.

Bailey and I both nodded when he asked whether the nurse had been in to check my bandages.

The doctor pointed to the empty bed beside mine. "Business has been slow. Enjoy your privacy."

"I still can't believe Donovan took those photos," I groaned after he left the room.

"She didn't," Bailey said. "That's why she came by the store. To tell you that she did some investigating of her own and discovered that Ricky Wilkinson took the photographs. Apparently he was standing outside the window between courses. He sold them to the highest bidder."

Closing my eyes, I sighed, "I never liked that kid." Trying hard to stay awake, I asked, "So if it's not Danni Donovan, then what's been eating at you?"

Bailey leaned over and kissed me gently on the cheek. "It can wait," she whispered.

When I opened my eyes again, Richard Morrell was seated in the chair where Bailey had been, his legs up, his ankles crossed on the edge of my bed.

"How ya feelin', *kemosabe*?" he asked.

"I've been better," I answered. "What's this crap about finding me below the snowmobile bridge?"

"Wasn't sure you wanted the world to know what had happened up there at the pond." Richard grinned. "Besides, my people never like to leave a trail for the cavalry to follow."

I stared down at the Wabanaki's black leather work boots.

Morrell shifted his legs off the bed. Walking across the room, he closed the door.

"I'm only telling you this because I settled my case with the paper company."

Pain racked my chest when I pushed up on my hands and adjusted my back against the pillows. My head felt like it might explode into little pieces, splattering blood, bone and flesh across the far wall. "So it was you been tearing down all those signs?"

"I may have started it, but near the end some of the old-timers got into the spirit of things." The Native American grabbed the remote from a bureau by the bed and clicked on the television that hung from the wall. Turning up the volume, he walked over to my side.

"Figured I'd have the roads to myself in a hurricane. Was heading up to the Kennebagos to take down some signs Wagner had put back up when I spotted you following the Silverado. After hearing about the pot farm, I thought you might need some backup. Trouble was, that damn tree came down behind your truck. I had to use my chainsaw to clear it from the road, and then it took a while to figure where you'd gotten to. By the time I pulled up to your Toyota and humped it down to the pond, that fella was pointing his *pistola* at you."

"So that was you in the bear suit?"

"*C'était moi.*" Morrell switched through the channels until he found one reporting on the weather.

"But I saw you take two in the chest." I remembered seeing him sprawled across the ground.

Swollen rivers and blown-down trees flashed across the screen while the commentator called Angie the worst hurricane to hit the western part of the state since they began keeping records.

"Another old Indian trick," he said. Morrell let a moment go by before delivering the punch line. "Bulletproof vest."

"But—"

He didn't wait for me to finish.

"I've been dressing up in that bear outfit in case one of the wardens got onto my trail. Ronnie came close up along the north shore of Mooselookmeguntic. That's when I got to thinking that some yahoo might decide to take a bear out of season. Hence a bit of battle rattle brought back from the Sandbox."

I must have looked puzzled because he added, "Been wearing a vest I borrowed from a guy who was on leave from Iraq. Although I've got to tell you, you're not the only one hurtin'." Morrell pulled aside his shirt to reveal two bruises, one red welt on his chest, the other lower down on his stomach. "Even with the Kevlar, it took the wind out of me," he added.

The weatherman on the television was forecasting fair skies for the next week.

"So what happened to the guy with the gun?" I asked.

"You mean the handsome dude?"

I nodded my head. Morrell looked toward the door and then lowered his voice.

"After I slammed into him, Mr. Good-Looking fell backward into the pond. By then, the other guy had sunk out of sight. You were lying in the mud, blood seeping onto the ground. My options were pretty limited. I mean, I didn't have time to do much of anything, except get you back to my truck. It took a couple of hours to drive down to Farmington, and by the time I got back up to the pond both of them were, well, they were gone. I assume the bog just drug 'em down."

He was silent for a moment, and then said, "After that, I drove back to town and picked up Rusty. The two of us cleaned up the scene and drove your truck down past the snowmobile bridges. Rusty hotwired the Silverado and I followed him over to the other side of the Kennebago Divide. Left it down an abandoned two-track deep in the forest. It'll take months, maybe years, before anyone finds it. We told those two state detectives we found you below the bridges. That you must have been shot by a hunter's stray bullet." The Wabanaki clicked off the remote.

"A hunter? In June? In a hurricane?"

"Hey, it was the best I could do under the circumstances. I don't think they bought it any more than your lame-ass story about how those guys got taken out at the pot farm, but after the hurricane, they can CSI all they want. They ain't finding shit."

I must have dozed off for a few minutes. When I awoke, Morrell was still sitting beside the bed. He held up a straw so I could drink from a plastic glass.

Licking my lips, I said, "Anyone else asking questions?"

"Whit dropped by with Lester to talk to the doctor. So did Ronnie, but the bullet went through you and they ain't gonna locate it where we said we found you. The state police will have more questions, but keep to our story, and well, I don't see any need to explain about the backpack."

I'd forgotten about the backpack.

Morrell ran a hand through his thick black hair. "We checked out your cabin and it looks none the worse for wear, although your friend's camp got battered pretty bad. Buried the backpack in a hole I dug under the small canoe beside that big pine by the pond, just in case one of those detectives got curious and decided to check out your place."

Just then the door opened.

"Time for your medicine." The nurse walked past Richard and handed me a number of different-colored pills.

Chapter Twenty-nine

The hurricane had damaged some of the equipment needed to complete the movie, but besides causing a brief delay, the storm had no other impact on Magalini's masterpiece or the town of Easie.

I returned to the cabin after my discharge from the hospital. Bailey insisted on spending the week caring for me, while Karen Ross looked after the bookstore.

Promising to be available for further questioning, Holly returned to her university. The day after my release from the hospital the two state detectives pulled down the lane to my cabin. They took turns grilling me until Bailey shooed them away. Convinced I knew more than I was telling them, they remained skeptical.

The following afternoon, Junior Ross stopped by. He told us three others, all part of Joe Hawley's grounds crew, were picked up. According to Whitney, each was more eager than the next to rat the others out. Junior had heard a rumor that two men associated with the film were reported missing, with the authorities searching the region for them. Ronnie had told him that the police asked the wardens' assistance in locating a black Silverado that was said to belong to one of the men.

"It's as if they vanished into thin air," the mechanic remarked before leaving.

It was nearing the end of that first week. Bailey and I sat in rockers on the porch, looking out over Otter Pond while waiting for Rusty and Jeanne Miller, with whom we planned to spend the afternoon. The temperature had climbed into the low eighties, but the hurricane had cleared out the humidity that had plagued us before its arrival. With warmer temperatures, most sports were returning to their homes, leaving both fish and fishing guides to enjoy the summer months.

I was having trouble getting around on my own, with an arm in a sling and my chest bandaged. Although the ache in my head had not subsided, it was less severe. Bailey seemed to have broken out of her funk and I decided to let sleeping dogs lie when she didn't volunteer an explanation for her previous behavior. Speaking of sleeping dogs, Buck and Rose lay on their sides, basking in the afternoon sun that streamed through the screens of the porch while Bailey and I sipped lemonade she had made from fresh lemons.

Ice jingled against the sides as I lowered the tall glass onto the green table between the rockers. Bailey helped me to my feet when I struggled to rise. With my good hand, I grabbed the binoculars that hung from the spruce notch and glassed the far side of the pond.

Adjusting the lens, I focused on a large doe that strutted out of the forest. A moment later, a single fawn appeared. As her mother trotted toward the edge of the pond, the second fawn broke through the line of spruce, joining her twin, the two young deer jumping and bucking in the high grass that had grown green and lush since their birth.

"Check it out." I handed the binoculars to Bailey. "Born a little over a month ago."

"They look so fragile," she replied.

"You'd be surprised." I was beginning to believe the two young deer might beat the odds.

"I've been waiting for the right time." Bailey hesitated. There were tears in her eyes when she lowered her glasses.

"I hope I can be as good a mother as that doe." She turned in my direction.

It took a moment for me to understand. Reaching out with my good arm, I tipped over the tall glass, ice cubes clattering onto the porch floor.

While the two dogs licked up the lemonade, Bailey explained that she hadn't wanted to concern me after the home test, at first waiting for the doctor to check for abnormalities, and after that, struggling with the idea of having a child at her age. Deciding to have the baby, Bailey delayed telling me after seeing the photograph with Danni Donovan, all the while worrying that I might not want a child, waiting for the right time that never seemed to come.

Drawing her close, I whispered that nothing would make me happier. Since I didn't have champagne at the cabin, we settled for refills of our lemonade, celebrating the news with the Millers when they arrived. I wanted to tell the world, but because of her age, Bailey made me promise to wait, swearing us to secrecy.

Later that afternoon, I breaded and fried some especially thin chicken cutlets Ollie Stubbs had reserved for me, adding a thin strip of mozzarella cheese to each and pouring over them Italian sauce prepared using my mother's recipe. While helping me with the dishes, Jeanne had whispered that her husband hadn't taken a drink since the day she collapsed into his arms.

Around dusk, I motioned for Rusty, who followed me out the door. We walked down to the pond followed by the two dogs. He looked better than I'd seen him in months, his hair cut and combed, his face shaved, the rufous mustache that drooped down over his upper lip neatly trimmed. He explained that the bank had commenced foreclosure proceedings. I was about to tell him about what had happened at the pond when he bent to one knee.

Finding a flat stone, he said, "I don't want to know."

Rusty skipped a stone across the pond. It was the first time we were alone since he had helped Richard Morrell remove any evidence of what had happened on Cupsuptic Pond.

I didn't say anything while watching the rock skip across the surface.

Bending forward, I grabbed a backpack that was jammed into the bow of my short canoe. When I handed it to Rusty, he asked, "What's this?"

Turning back up the path, I replied, "You said you didn't want to know."

Chapter Thirty

Father Brendan smiled, his teeth as white as the edge along a brook trout's fin.

"Sal-va-torrrre," he called as I backed my truck down the public boat launch between Hawley's Marina and Koz's Garage. As previously agreed, the priest had walked up from Our Lady of the Lakes, the stone church around the corner from the Wooden Nickel and a few blocks away from Lakewood Sports.

"On a morning such as this we are all believers, wouldn't you say, Sal-va-torrrre?"

I grunted a noncommittal response while removing the straps around the Grumman. My chest hurt when I pulled the boat off the trailer. Across Hawley Pond, boats crisscrossed under the early-morning sun.

It was unseasonably warm for the last week of September and although it was not quite nine in the morning, the younger man wore the sleeves of a black-and-white checkered flannel shirt rolled to his elbows. He had unbuckled the shoulder straps of his chest waders, allowing them to drape down over a belt around his waist.

The priest held a rod tube in his left hand as he walked down to the water's edge. I carried the little cane rod recently purchased during a weekend at the Bethel Inn. Taking no chances, I had slung over my shoulder a larger rucksack that contained a few tools and spare parts should the engine break down, rain gear if the weather might change, a first aid kit in case either of us sustained an injury, and a roll of duct tape for any other emergency that might befall us. But with the sun warm on the back of my neck, it was hard to think about emergencies. Instead, as the pain in my chest subsided, I smiled at the thought of all those bends in the river yet to be explored with Bailey and of all the stories still to be told to our child.

Junior Ross trotted down from the station as Brendan took his place in the bow. The young man stood at the end of the wooden dock while I organized our gear. When he asked where we were headed I told him that a gentleman never tells. Another flash of pain seared through my chest when I pulled on the outboard's cord, slowly subsiding as the engine putt-puttered into action. Slipping the gear out of neutral, I steered the Grumman away from the ramp.

A week earlier, a bear hunter had stumbled across the Silverado, Arthur Wentworth, Sr. confessing to his involvement in the pot farm after the state lab confirmed trace amounts of marijuana along with Arthur's fingerprints in the vehicle. Although he insisted he had no information regarding the whereabouts of LeBron Hayes or the Michael Douglas look-alike, Arthur implicated them in the crime. Not long afterward, Whitney stopped by to tell me that I was no longer a person of interest. Although the search continued for the two missing men, the investigation into the pot farm and my shooting had been closed.

The young doctor was right about my hard head. By the middle of August I had fully recovered from the residual headaches, dizziness and ringing that had come and gone in the weeks that followed my release from the hospital. My elbow no longer gave me trouble and the wound under my eye had healed, leaving only a faint scar.

Although the bullet wound had also healed, the doctor cautioned that for the next six months my chest would compete with my hip and back for my attention. Even so, he said I was a lucky man.

As we motored up the west shoreline, I waved to Bailey, who, although six months pregnant, barely showed as she stood on the deck of the apartment above the bookstore. Beside her, asleep in the sun, Buck lay on his side while Rose stood at attention wagging her tail.

"God truly works in mysterious ways," the Nigerian-born priest proclaimed as we motored past the rear of the Millers' sporting goods store.

Jeanne walked out of the back door carrying a mug of coffee to her husband, who was hosing down their Grady White, the fiberglass boat they used to guide sports on the big pond. Jeanne had kept Bailey's secret while Rusty had kept mine.

"How so?" I asked, steering past the outlet of the Hawley River.

"Mr. Miller inheriting all that money from his aunt. I mean, what are the chances? And just in time to pay off their debt and stop the foreclosure? I'd say the good Lord was looking out for them."

I slid a hand over my chest. Looking down at the cane rod, I smiled. "Not to mention this little baby sitting in the window of that fly shop all winter. Surely it would have been sold to someone else if not for Divine intervention."

The priest slapped his knee. Laughing loudly, he said, "Make jokes, my friend. We may not know his plan, but the Shepherd provides for his sheep."

Leaving the town behind, I cruised up the pond. In no particular hurry, I slowly worked my way toward the headwaters that flowed out of the mountains separating Maine from Canada. I pointed to an immature loon while explaining to the priest how the bird's parents would be joining other adults, soon to leave for the coast, where they'd spend the winter on the ocean.

Most years, Brendan would have shipped back to Africa before the September spawning runs of salmon and trout, but the previous week the Monsignor's appendix had burst, leaving the Nigerian in charge until the other priest was back on his feet.

"But what will happen to the little bloke?" he asked, referring to the young loon that hadn't lost its gray plumage.

"He'll wait for as long as he can, practicing flying, which doesn't come easy to a loon, finding his own way to the sea just before ice forms on the pond."

"Mysterious ways, Sal-va-torrrre, mysterious ways." The priest's smile was infectious.

Father Brendan pointed over my left shoulder. Turning, I watched an eagle glide along a thermal current, the big bird sweeping up and over the hills to the southwest. I knew that eagles preyed on immature loons, but decided not to impart that information to the good Father.

"You know, Sal-va-torrrre, the Church needs soldiers in its battle against evil. When will I see you at Our Lady of the Lakes?"

Sweeping my arm out in front of me, I said, "This is all the church I need."

We motored into a small cove where weeds wavered just under the tannin-stained water. The outboard would overheat if the long tendrils tangled around its propeller, and I steered closer to shore, prompting a small flock of Canada geese to take flight.

Richard Morrell stood on a hill above the bank. On a nearby tree, a sign identified the logging road where he had parked his truck. According to Junior Ross, as part of the Wabanaki's settlement, Baybrook had hired him to patrol its roads, the other paper companies soon following suit. When Richard waved his arm, I saw the Wagner Forest Management patch stitched on his sleeve.

A few minutes later, we motored around a bend that opened into a large expanse of water. Tall grass grew on mud flats that extended out into the pond from the western shoreline while on the east bank the conifer forest grew down to the water's edge. Motoring through the cove, we entered a deep channel and then ran up a set of shallow riffles that tumbled down out of Little Hawley Brook. I lifted the outboard to avoid hitting the bed of cobble that stood out in the clear water. Climbing out of the stern, I waded along the side of the Grumman and with my good arm pulled the bow onto a pebbly shoal.

While recuperating, I had played around with a new streamer pattern, one tied with a body of pale blue silk over white thread and ribbed with silver tinsel.

The wing consisted of four dun-colored hen hackles over a few strands of white buck tail and peacock herl. While still at the boat, I knotted the streamer to the priest's tippet. Wading toward the channel, I explained that more often than not, a salmon might strike on the first cast.

Father Brendan took my advice to heart. As I took a knee beside him, the priest slid his sunglasses over his eyes, the brim of his cap low on his brow. With a look of concentration across his dark features, he cast into the current. Halfway across the channel, a fish rolled under the sunlit surface. The next moment the silver-and-black flash leaped skyward. As he turned in my direction, my sport's smile was as broad as the bend in his rod, but before I could rise to my feet, the fish had slipped the priest's hook.

Shrugging his shoulders, Father Brendan turned back toward the run. Over the next couple of hours, he worked his way up the channel, taking a few small fish by lunchtime.

I heated a cast iron pan over a twig fire. While frying a few pork chops in the juice from a jar of marinated peppers, I cut up an onion and stirred in the slices with the peppers. As sun splashed down around us, we joked about Magalini's movie, wondering whether it would do justice to my daughter's novels. As we ate the streamside lunch, our conversation slipped back and forth between matters philosophical and those piscatorial, the priest taking the latter as seriously as the former.

It had been an exceptionally pleasant day, with a slight breeze out of the west and temperatures in the low seventies. Brendan looked toward the north, where the clouds loomed large. Although still in the distance, they had formed immense thunderheads.

The Nigerian's smile was a testament to his unflinching belief in the goodness of the Creator. "Glorious, don't you think?" he whispered in an almost reverential tone. "Like heavenly turrets spiraling up from God's kingdom."

I flipped down my sunglasses. Now at our backs, the sun shifted toward the west, where it resisted the efforts of the large mass of cloud to overtake it. The sky that loomed above us reminded me of a painting by Tiziano Vecellio, the sixteenth-century Italian painter better known as Titian.

A small fish flickered over the pond's rubescent surface. Looking over my shoulder, I called to the good-natured priest, who waded in my direction.

Rises now dimpled the water. Casting toward the nearest set of concentric circles, Father Brendan soon held a small finger-size trout in his palm.

On his next cast, another char slapped the water, held fast to the little wet fly I had exchanged for the streamer. A third fish, and then a fourth, followed. The sunlight made each appear like a tongue of flame.

I was thinking that if the wild was my religion, these hills, this water, must surely be my church, but set aside the thought when the surface fell away from under the priest's fly. With the sound of my sport's reel filling my ear, I waded back toward the Grumman to grab my two-handed net.

Lucky man indeed.